Sweet Raptor Jesus!

Published by Camilla Monk

Cover design by Camilla Monk

ISBN: 978-1-64316-081-8

APACHE STRIKE FORCE

A SPOTLESS NOVELLA

CAMILLA MONK

TABLE OF CONTENTS

This book is dedicated to you, dear reader.
Take this modest offering of pointless fluff as a token of my gratitude.

ONE
THE EYE OF SIMON

"The aircraft ripped through the night air as he went full throttle. Whoever fucking dared to hurt Chanterelle better get ready to fucking die."

–Samara Frost, *SEALcopter #1 - Blades of Love*

That phone call went all sorts of wrong. Although, in retrospect, I'm not sure what I expected: I had been missing for eight months, possibly dead to all who loved me, and one fine morning in December, I just called my dad out of the blue. It was 7:00 a.m. in New York, he hadn't even had breakfast yet, and there I was, sobbing at the other end of the line, struggling to form words. I was in Paris; I was okay; I wanted to come home to him.

"Island, Island, honey, is that you? Oh God, are you okay? Are you wounded? What happened? Is there someone with you? What the hell *happened*?"

I had no intelligible answer to my dad's subsequent barrage of questions, no strength left to keep my own emotions under control and reassure him. I tried to speak, but only hiccups would come out, and wiping my nose with the sleeve of my fleece pj's didn't seem to help. That's when a former hit man known to most as March, who had just gotten out of bed at 1:00 p.m., came to the rescue. I hadn't even noticed him entering the living room. He was wearing nothing but a pair of dark boxer shorts; he must have woken up when he heard me crying. I found myself cocooned into a safe haven of bed-warmed skin and springy chest hair as he carefully took the phone from my shaking hands.

March barely had the time to say, "Good morning, Mr. Halder," before my father exploded. "Who the hell are you? What have you done to my daughter? Island! Where are they holding you? I swear I'll—"

"Please calm down, Mr. Halder. Island is perfectly safe—"

"How much do you want?" my father barked.

His outburst only made me wail harder. "Dad, I swear I'm okay! Please, listen!"

"Don't worry, honey! It's gonna be okay; I'm gonna find you! And you"—I gathered that growl was for March—"I'm gonna find you too! And I'm not Liam Neeson, but if you touch a single hair on her head, the last thing you'll see is—"

March gave the slightest wince at the rage-fueled rant pouring from the speaker. "I understand . . . but I can assure you I'm not holding Island hostage."

"Let me speak to her!"

With a big gulp of air, I managed to hold back my tears long enough to take the phone from March's hands. "Please, calm down and listen to me. I'm not being held hostage or anything."

March's palm squeezed my shoulder in silent encouragement. I swallowed hard to steady my voice. "Like I said, I'm in Paris, and I'm okay now. I promise."

"Who's that man with you?" my dad probed, before his breath caught, and his voice cracked into a near sob. "Honey, they told me you were *dead*! I *need* to understand what happened."

"He's . . . his name is March." I gulped as a year-old memory resurfaced, of Joy catching March as he was busy roping me on my bed with my own tights. The keywords summing up this dreadful incident could be: *misunderstanding* and *BDSM*. "Joy told you about him . . . back when he took me to Paris for the first time." I winced and refrained from adding: *Remember? He's my forty-year-old dom.*

Of course my dad remembered.

This time, an unbearable silence stretched between us. I could almost see the various bricks of partial data, parental prejudice, and mild paranoia organize themselves in his brain as he murmured, "Did you . . . run away with him?"

"No! I was . . . look, something happened at the Poseidon . . . It's very complicated, and I don't want to do this over the phone."

"*Oh Jesus . . . Jesus . . .*" I felt his ragged sigh in the speaker as if it were my own, and I had to blink hard no to burst into tears all over again.

I knew I had already said too much and not nearly enough, that every missing piece of the puzzle was absolute torture to him, but I couldn't tell him like this, over the phone, that I had been kidnapped, brainwashed, drugged, nearly lobotomized . . . It was too difficult to put in words with 3,600 miles between us, so all I said was, "Please. Trust me. I can . . . I mean, I'll jump on a plane as soon as—"

March stepped in before I was even done talking. "Island, it's too early. Your wound—"

"What *wound*? What is he talking about?" And with this, my dad was panicking tenfold.

I had almost forgotten about it, but as if on cue, a zing of pain at the back of my skull reminded me that there was still a rather large patch of hair missing and a one-inch-long cut there. My stitches were now dry and clean, but it'd be at least another ten days before they fell off.

"Well, I got"—I bit my lower lip. He wasn't going to like this—"I got a little brain surgery."

A renewed string of breathless cussing reached me through the speaker. "*Jesus fucking Christ . . .* Baby, baby, what *happened*?"

My lips parted to answer, but words failed me. For a couple of seconds, I just stood still in the middle of that quiet, impersonal Parisian living room, my gaze lost past the windows and the gray weather outside. I looked up to find March's tired and attentive blue gaze seeking mine.

Memories collided in my newly awakened brain, good and bad, as I contemplated trying to explain to my dad how some mad Norwegian scientist had been ordered by my supervillain uncle to put a neuroelectrical implant in my brain to shoot my long-term memory and how they'd locked me up and drugged me for eight months, before March came to save me in an ice-cream truck that fired rockets, and seven days ago, that same implant had been removed, thanks to the very turd who had been overseeing my captivity all this time. Also, I'd been to space. To stop the aforementioned uncle from firing a nuclear missile at Earth. There'd been a sloth . . . and Dries, my biological father . . . was dead.

No. It was too early for a detailed account of my recent adventures. I needed to ease my dad into all this. And maybe I needed time too. Everything was too fresh, too vivid, and already, I could feel knots form in my throat as I tried to put words on what I'd been through. "I'll tell you everything," I eventually said. "But I need a little time."

I thought he'd explode again and insist on knowing everything, but he just said, "Wait for me, honey. I'm coming."

That sudden gravity, the renewed strength in my father's voice, those made me realize how much I needed him right now. "Okay, I'll be waiting."

"Island, honey?"

I sniffed. "Yes?"

"Can I speak to . . . *March*?"

I gritted my teeth and gripped the phone a little harder in response.

You see, back when I was a teen and went to live with him after my mom's death, it took me less than a couple of weeks to realize that this father of mine, who sent me Mickey Mouse postcards and cutting-edge gaming consoles for my birthday, belonged, in fact, to a different species than my mom. She was an adept of what you might call . . . free-range parenting. As in: "I'll be away for the rest of the week; you call that trattoria down the street to order your meals. Love you, *chérie*."

Now my dad . . . Did you watch reruns of *Airwolf* when you were a kid? I did, and I wanted Jan-Michael Vincent to marry me and take me away in his supersonic helicopter, and we'd fire at the bad guys with the chain guns and blow up enemies with our rockets. What I'm trying to say is that the first time I saw my dad explode at a math teacher who had dared to slam me with a C- for sustaining that Descartes's equiangular spiral equation could be used to predict the size of a giant, man-eating nautilus, I came to realize that mine was an authentic helicopter dad. Hovering, droning above school personnel, orthodontists, and shop assistants alike, ready to fire at the first offense. I learned to anticipate his outbursts and associate them with *Airwolf*'s theme: the rotor would start spinning slowly, then faster and faster, in tune with heroic background music, before a random Jeep on the ground exploded in a blaze of flames and smoke.

And so, as my dad waited for me to hand the phone to March, I could hear the low hum of the rotor, gaining speed. I gulped.

"Island?" my dad insisted.

March's lips moved to form a silent, *It's all right.*

I feared it would be everything but, and I'm somewhat ashamed to recall that he had to pry the phone from my hands when I raised it: my fingers wouldn't let go . . .

"Mr. November speaking."

As soon as March's deeper timbre replaced mine, my father's voice went down to a threatening hiss. I caught the words *jail* and *FBI* amid what sounded like a slew of gruesome threats.

"It's all right, Mr. Halder," March replied, his voice even—no doubt because the slightest hint of cordiality might be interpreted by my dad as taunting and would inevitably lead to another round of fire. "Please do contact the FBI, and ask for Mr. Clifford Murrell, who recently joined the International Operations Division. I believe he'll be able to confirm that Island is not currently being held against her will."

My jaw probably hit the floor at the same time as my dad's. He went silent for a few seconds, allowing March to go on. "Of course, since you don't trust a word of what I'm saying, first you're going to call Attorney General Matthew Jensen, who graduated with you from Harvard and heads the National Security Division. He will no doubt look up Mr. Murrell for you and confirm his identity. Once you've spoken to Mr. Murrell, my assistant will contact you to arrange a private flight to Paris at your earliest convenience."

Okay. He had prepared for this. Like, *really* prepared. I stared at March wide-eyed while, on the other end of the line, my father remained speechless. He was probably thinking he had been dragged into one of those thriller plots where mysterious assholes call you out of nowhere and seem to already know everything about you. "Island," he said hesitantly. "Is she still there? Let me talk to her."

"Of course." March gave me back the phone with a little wink.

My dad drew a few feverish breaths before he asked me in a near whisper. "Honey. I need to know . . . is he dangerous?"

I decided that if March was going to be part of our lives for the foreseeable future, honesty was the only viable policy. Looking up at the interested party with a tenderness I could feel warming my chest and easing the tension in my limbs, I answered, "No, he's not dangerous—not to you and me."

TWO
THE LABELS

"Honestly, some hobbies are best left unshared. Make sure to
check yours against our list on page 145."

—Aurelia Nichols & Jillie Bean, *101 Tips to Lock Him Down*

Sitting cross-legged in an oversize velvet armchair, I held my head still as a young doctor examined my pupils with a penlight. He'd shown up not long after my dad had hung up with a final promise to come for me as soon as possible. Uncharacteristically, March had retreated to the bedroom after welcoming the doctor, to take a call from Phyllis. I was pretty sure those two were monitoring my dad's every move on top of organizing his flight to Paris. I knew March and his omnipotent assistant meant well, but I'd probably need to have a chat with him about not tapping my family's phones, at some point. Mine? Let's be real: if I forbade March to geolocate it to his heart's content, I'd probably end up with a tracker stuck to my underwear label instead . . .

"Have you eaten yet?" the doctor asked with an unmistakable creole accent—guy must have been from Guadeloupe or Martinique.

"Sort of," I replied. "Does applesauce count?"

He chuckled. "Yes. Any pain?"

"My stitches hurt a little, but the rest of my head is actually fine. I honestly thought I'd wake up with the worst migraine of my life."

His lips quirked. "Give it a little time."

"Great . . ."

He shrugged. "Your post-op MRI showed no trace of bleeding. I'm writing you a prescription for painkillers. Only take some if you need it: it's not candy," he warned while scribbling something on a prescription pad.

"I get it." I watched him close his case and grab his coat and scarf from the couch. "Can I go out?"

His head lolled in indecision. "Make sure the wound remains clean and covered. Eat something first, and take it easy. Parc Astérix is off the menu."

"I wasn't thinking of that," I replied with an uneasy laugh. *Dammit*, was this practitioner of the shadows reading my mind?

"Thank you, doctor. I'll make sure she stays away from roller coasters for the time being."

I hopped from the armchair to find March standing in the living room doorway—one of the minor inconveniences of having a boyfriend equipped with a stealth mode. I had yet to leave my pajamas, but he had changed into a pair of jeans and one of his magic crease-free white shirts half an hour ago to welcome the doctor. How one could possibly freshen up, shave, and properly button their shirt in less than ten minutes, I would never know: March was a black belt at adulting, having mastered grooming techniques and organizational skills a grasshopper such as myself could barely comprehend—much less emulate.

"What about flying?" I asked the doctor while he shrugged on his coat.

He frowned. "Long-haul, I suppose?"

I nodded.

"Normally, this is the part where I tell you to go back to bed and stay there for at least another couple of days."

I gave him an imploring look.

"But you are, *technically*, stable enough to fly."

I turned to March with a victorious grin, but he didn't seem fully convinced: his gaze searched the doctor's, waiting for the additional warning that would warrant dragging me back under the comforter. But the guy only shook his head with a sympathetic smile that seemed to translate as, "You're on your own, dude."

After the apartment's reinforced-steel door had slammed shut, I latched on to March. "So . . . did my dad call Murrell?"

His lips curved into one of the rare smiles I knew were for me only, pinching two dimples. "Yes. Your father was quite unhappy with the answers he was given and made sure everyone he spoke to was well aware of that."

I winced. "What did they tell him?"

"Nothing. The entire *Odysseus* file is classified, much like yours, mine, and everything pertaining to the Lions."

Odysseus . . . I thought of the half-destroyed space station, a huge white ring orbiting 250 miles above us in the immensity of space. A cold tomb for the man who had killed my mother eleven years ago—and also for quite a few of his men, in the wake of March's first space adventure. "What will they tell everyone?"

"They're denying that any launch took place in Ecuador, and the official report will conclude that a major depressurization incident in the orbital ring killed all crew members."

Yeah, you could call it that. March had definitively "depressurized" those treacherous astronauts and Anies's Lions one by one. Anies himself though . . . my hand still prickled at the memory of holding the knife, plunging it into his side, so fast, so easily. I had only meant to defend myself, but in the end, I had killed him. And closed the circle. It didn't really feel like revenge for my parents' deaths, even though it *was*. More like another life wasted, more blood, and that queasiness I could feel returning in the pit of my stomach.

March stepped closer, trailing his knuckles against my cheek. "I'm sorry . . . biscuit. For everything."

I kissed his palm. "It's okay. I guess it'll just take me a little longer than the US government to put a lid on all this."

"I know . . . Your father should land in eight hours. That leaves you a little longer to rest before—"

"All hell breaks loose?" I chuckled.

"I foresee a long night," March admitted with a sigh.

I leaned closer for a hug, nuzzling his chest. "Do you want to tell him . . . everything?" About *Odysseus*, and what had happened to me, of course, but also . . . about March's former line of employment.

"Do you want me to?" he asked quietly.

He would, I realized. If I asked him, March would tear down that last wall between us, the secrecy that was his fortress. I shook my head. "I can't ask you to do that. I'll go with whatever you decide to tell him. We can say you work for the CIA, something like that."

He rested his chin atop my head. "I understand." A sigh breezed in my hair. "I doubt he'll content himself with elusive answers though."

"Yeah, he can be kinda . . . relentless."

"He found Struthio's LinkedIn page and sent me an invitation."

I smiled against his shirt. "*Oh God . . .* Already?"

"And he asked Phyllis if I could provide my résumé, along with copies of my degrees and tax returns," March added, a smile in his voice.

"I'm really sorry . . ." I squeezed my eyes shut. Just imagining the amount of lies awaiting me made my forehead throb unpleasantly. March's education? Should I make up something, or weather the storm as I revealed to my dad that the love of my life had dropped from school at fifteen, and I couldn't have cared less? Tax returns? Oh, March had those. Over the course of his career, he had made a point to scrupulously fulfill his taxpayer duties, whether in South Africa or the US. All that was left to explain was that those millions he'd declared had been made . . . as a hit man.

"Don't worry," March purred. "Handling our return to civilization can't be more difficult than flying to space."

"Honestly . . . I'm not sure I'm ready. I need to see him, and I know I also have to call Joy, take care of a million things to wrestle my life back in order, but"—I let out a shivering sigh—"all I want to do is . . . escape."

He stroked a hand down my back. "When this is over for good, I'll take you anywhere you want, and we'll behave irresponsibly . . . for at least a week."

I giggled. "Netflix and chill every night?"

His lips trailed to my ear shell, and a delicate nip made my toes curl. "Chill, mostly."

That sent a different kind of shiver dancing up my spine. "I'll hold you to that, Mr. November. Chill. Every. Night," I whispered. "But until then . . . I think I'm gonna take a shower."

"All right. You should have everything you need in the bathroom, but let me know if anything is missing."

I rubbed my hands in anticipation. "Phyllis struck again?"

He nodded pensively. "Unlike me, she appears to understand the nuance between a smoothing shampoo and conditioner."

"Don't worry; I'm not entirely sure either. But I like to read the ingredients to find out how they make it. Did you know they put powdered-mica nanoparticles to imitate gold in glittery makeup? Labels are a world of entertainment at hand's reach."

March's mouth pursed in agreement. "You're preaching to a converted. I actually went through a phase where I collected can labels as a child. I grew out of it toward the age of fourteen, but I still enjoy looking up products on the USDA's food-composition database. A fascinating tool."

If someone had barged into the living room with a camera and taken a pic of me at the precise second he said this, they would have seen the face of love, no, *adoration*. It was because of tiny moments like this that I measured how goddamn lucky I was. We came from opposite worlds, had grown up thousands of miles and almost a decade apart. Like two grains of sand in the ocean—who both enjoyed reading labels and Wikipedia—what were the statistical chances that fate would entwine our paths? No . . . it wasn't luck. Dries had accomplished that. Because he'd spawned me and taken March under his wing. Without even being aware of it at the time, he had created a world of possibilities, and now he was gone, but *we* remained.

"Island?"

March's face looked concerned and a little blurry as I phased back in. I wiped my eyes with the back of my hand, and he cradled my cheeks in his palms right afterward, stroking them with his thumbs. "What's on your mind, biscuit?"

"Yeah. I just . . . I was thinking we wouldn't have met if it hadn't been for Dries."

He pulled me to him and hugged me tight, just like I needed. "I know."

"Does he . . ." My voice caught, before I managed to force the words out. "Will he be buried somewhere?"

March's sigh breezed in my hair. "Erwin's men probably recovered his body from Saraya, but I doubt the CIA will return it. I'm sorry, Island."

"It's okay. I kind of figured it'd be like that."

"But there's a family grave in Johannesburg. He and Anies staged their burial there, when they joined the Lions. I can take you someday, if you'd like."

"Yes, please. Even if he's not resting there . . . I think I'd like to have a place where to say goodbye."

"I understand."

I let the wave of sadness wash over me, anchored by March's arms around me, and after a while, I felt strong enough to let go of him. "Okay," I said, balling my fists. "I've got some labels to read."

•••

Someone needed to write Chanel to tell them that coumarin was potentially toxic, and they shouldn't put that in their shower gel. I told March so while slipping on a pair of black velvet skinny pants and a beige turtleneck I had found waiting for me in the bedroom's closet. He agreed that we should write them to complain—it was one of his many couponing strategies, and he assured me that a well-worded complaint would earn us, at the very least, a few samples. We might even get free products, were I to claim that I'd actually experienced dire side effects from all that coumarin.

Honestly, I was fine, but March looked up from his phone as he typed, studied my face, and said I looked very pale. He then returned to his typing, pressed send, and somewhere in France a "Customer Care Representative" got an e-mail from a guy who claimed that their shower gel had potentially poisoned his girlfriend, and as a result, he demanded samples and coupons in reparation.

After he was done, March tipped his head to the gray sky outside and the spire of Notre-Dame, shrouded in afternoon fog. "I should probably keep you in bed, but something tells me only handcuffs could possibly achieve that. So, perhaps I could take you to see Kalahari and Ilan. I think they'll be very happy to see you awake and . . . yourself again."

I battled the urge to jump up and down at March's mention of his awesome ex and her husband, still worried that my stitches might somehow reopen and cause an unexpected brain leakage. "Oh *yes*! I seriously need that. Also"—my stomach completed that sentence for me with a low gurgle. I patted it sadly—"do we have anything else other than applesauce? I'm starving."

"There's yogurt and some excellent potato-leek soup," March said. When he noticed my grimace of disappointment, he added, "You spent almost a week on a nutrition drip; the clinic recommended light and liquid meals for at least a couple of days, until your stomach is ready for a *reasonable* Christmas meal."

"No steak frites?"

"Not today," he confirmed with a sympathetic nod.

I briefly mourned the fact that I wouldn't be able to binge on croissants until I passed out as I'd initially planned, before my eyes went wide in realization. "Tomorrow . . . tomorrow's Christmas Eve."

March nodded.

So there was still a small chance that I'd be home for Christmas.

With my dad, Joy, and . . . A grin tugged at my cheeks. "It'll be our first Christmas together, you and me."

"True . . ."

"What do you normally do for Christmas?" I inquired while shrugging on a comfy navy wool coat and concealing my bald spot with a fleece beanie.

"Well," he began, putting on his own coat, "not much, to be honest. If I'm not working, I open a good bottle of whisky, and I watch Christmas specials with Gerald."

I recognized his answer for what it was: a tactful way to say that he drank alone for Christmas because, really, March had no family to go home to, save for a father he no longer spoke to because he held him responsible for his mother's overdose twenty years ago. The thought weighed painfully in my chest as I followed him in the elevator; I took his hand and squeezed it. The ancient grille clanked shut, and the car went down with ominous creaking sounds—we had four floors to go, and I silently prayed to Raptor Jesus that I wouldn't meet my demise in a poorly maintained elevator after having survived a two-hundred-mile free fall in a space pod with a crappy parachute.

"This year will be different," I announced when the doors (thankfully) opened. "We'll be together. We usually celebrate at my grandparents' house on Long Island." As soon as this quasi-invitation slipped past my lips, I hesitated and bit my tongue in an effort to shut up. Maybe I was going too fast?

March led me to a black Citroën SUV with tinted windows that was parked in the street. He flashed me a look of doubt while unlocking the doors. "It might perhaps be a little early for your father to welcome me into the family. At this point, all I'm hoping is that he won't try to file a restraining order against me."

"He'd never do that," I reassured him once we were both seated. *Okay, he totally would . . .* "Did you answer his LinkedIn invite, by the way?"

"Yes."

"Good . . . I think it'll help. He's really into it."

"I noticed. I went to like his article on unsecured bonds."

I studied his profile with no small amount of awe as the engine started, and he maneuvered us out of one of those tight parking jobs Parisians specialize in. "You've really thought this through, haven't you?"

"The supreme art of war is to subdue the enemy without fighting*," March concluded with a wink.

One could be forgiven for mistakenly attributing this quote to a morally bankrupt turd who liked Roomba cats and was known to a select few as Mr. Stiles. That's actually Sun Tzu speaking here.

THREE
PARASITOSIS

"Rhaow watched Manaha as she plunged in the river, the life-giving water washing away the mud to reveal her full curves. Manaha's breasts were pale and round, like the eggs of those-who-have-wings. His stick of joy ached with the need to shoot a child in her.'"

–Andrea Cherie, *Speared by the Caveman: A Prehistoric Romance*

Not even the hell that was Parisian traffic the day before Christmas Eve could have ruined this trip. But Lord, did it try. That girl with her shopping bags full of presents was lucky that March was a ruthless killer *and* a considerate road user, otherwise she might have finished that phone call under our wheels. With tightly set lips, he dodged Sushi Shop scooters and suicidal cyclists alike, along a ribbon of stone buildings and dead trees brought back to life by a multitude of string lights.

My forehead resting against the window, I drank in the sights around me, the shops inside which late shoppers hurried, the red and gold lights reflected on the glistening sidewalks, the threatening clouds above our heads . . . A light drizzle pattered outside as we followed the Seine all the way to Esplanade des Invalides. I thought of the first time I'd been there with March almost a year and a half ago, in a car too, but as his prisoner. I didn't trust him yet, back then. Because I had no idea who he truly was, everything that bound us. And now it felt so strange to be in that same place again, kind of like traveling back in time . . . I looked away from the Invalides's long grass parterres, to gaze at him. He didn't really notice: some douchenozzle in a Jaguar with a diplomatic plate that had been tailgating us for a while now cut him off, and he hit the brakes with a huff of aggravation.

"I'm sorry," March said. "We're almost there."

"It's okay." I peeked outside to see that the black Jaguar had unfortunately picked the wrong line to be a dick and was now stuck behind a garbage truck. "Here, let me fix this for you," I offered. I lowered my window and double flipped the driver as we drove past him, making sure to perform a slow, circular motion with my hands for extra damage.

"Biscuit . . ." March chided, his lips quirking nonetheless.

I raised my window back up with a firm nod. "Justice has been served."

He shook his head with a chuckle as the Eiffel tower came in sight, standing majestically at the end of Rue Saint-Dominique, half-shrouded in a pearly fog. We drove past clothing shops and bakeries whose colorful windows only acted as an excruciating reminder that I was expected to eat yogurt and soup today, until he took a turn right and stopped in front of a modern white building I recognized . . .

March turned off the engine and undid his seat belt but made no move to leave the car. Instead, he turned to face me and cupped my cheek tenderly, bringing my head closer to his. It reminded me of another kiss, long ago, one that didn't happen because a bum sprawled himself on our car's hood, and March nearly shot him until he realized the threat was fairly manageable.

But *this* kiss happened. He brushed his lips to mine, teasingly at first, pecking my Cupid's bow, before my mouth parted to ask for more. I tasted the familiar blend of coffee and mints on his tongue, losing myself in the moment. His lips tugged, warred with mine, and I clung to him, digging my fingers in his coat. March's breath grew ragged as his mouth trailed down to my chin and even lower, to nip at my neck. I kissed his hair, massaged his scalp with incoherent mewls of encouragement. It was so rare for him to let loose like that, and God, I didn't want him to regain control; I needed the high, that little spark of magic between us. One of my hands ventured between us, to his thigh, then higher, to show him just how welcome he was to bang me savagely in the car, between Ilan and Kalahari's building and a laundromat.

And he made me hope. Scratch that, he made me *dream*. Dammit, when he ground against my palm instead of removing my hand, and I felt his own hands sneak under my coat to grab my butt and pull me to him, I glimpsed my very first chance ever to behave like a lewd, irresponsible girl. And I said—gasped—"Yes!" repeatedly, but he . . . well, he sighed my name and pulled away.

I sat there like an idiot, shaking, breathless, a sheen of sweat beading on my forehead. "What was that for?" *And more importantly, why the hell did you have to stop?*

At least March appeared ruffled by our impromptu make out session too—a small consolation. He readjusted his clothes and pressed a chaste kiss to my hair, lingering a second to smell it. "I needed a little something to tide me over until I have you entirely to myself."

For a second there, I almost wanted to suggest we race back to the apartment and spend the rest of the day in bed instead of paying social calls like civilized human beings. I wanted to live the life of a bonobo. But I also wanted to see Kalahari and Ilan again, see the faces, hear the voices I thought I'd never remember. Then, in a few hours, my dad would land in Roissy, exhausted, worried sick, and it still wouldn't be the time for March and me to eat leaves naked—or engage in any kind of furious genital rubbing for that matter. I leaned into his touch, enjoying the heady rush of hormones lingering in my veins. "How you torment me, Mr. November . . ."

He ducked his head to conceal a grin. "As you do me, Miss Chaptal."

After a quick check in the mirror to make sure I didn't look—too much—like the profligate strumpet I longed to become, I followed March outside and into the building. I recognized the granite tiling, the no-smoking signs in the elevator Ilan probably purposefully ignored, and on the seventh and last floor, the single set of black doors at the end of a long hallway. They were already ajar, a discreet reminder that there was no need to ring or call: nothing escaped Ilan's former-spy eye. I felt suddenly nervous, out of place, as if the fourteen months since my last visit were a lifetime and maybe everything would be different.

To my relief, Ilan looked the same as I remembered when he opened the doors: a giant whose features were etched with deep lines, as if time, experience, and loss had raked his skin over and over until it became bronze leather. His sweatshirt and cargo pants were wrinkled and covered with crusty white stains, and I thought his green eyes seemed perhaps more tired than in my memories, but they came alive the moment he saw me. A warm grin split his face, and before I could say a word, he pulled me into a crushing hug. "Good to see you," he said, his voice gravelly from years—decades—of smoking. He didn't smell of cigarettes today though, I noted, as he let go of me to pat March's shoulder with a chuckle. "And here's the living legend."

I sent March a questioning look that he eluded with an uneasy smile.

"Where's Kalahari?" I asked, taking in the familiar gray designer furniture and pristine walls. Something had changed here that I couldn't quite place. Maybe it was a little messier than I remembered, with all those paper towels and meds on the coffee table.

"I'm here," a feminine voice called from down the hall leading to the bedrooms. A door opened, and when she appeared before us, there it was, that subtle change. A tiny parasite clung to her oversize jean shirt, drooling on the fabric. And she looked as beautiful as ever, but at the same time . . . really washed up. The same black as the creature's, her own curls had been hastily tied into a loose bun. Her yoga pants bore the same suspicious stains as Ilan's clothes did, and I had never seen her without any makeup or her mile-high heels.

But she radiated happiness as she walked to us. Keeping the baby—because it was one—firmly latched to her chest with a practiced hand, she extended the other to caress March's cheek in that tender, almost sensual, way I had misinterpreted the first time I had witnessed her do that. But it was a different kind of love, and I now felt it too as her fingers glided away from him to stroke my face much in the same way. Her touch was tentative at first, her fingertips quivering as if she couldn't believe it was me. I inhaled deeply her flowery perfume, mingled with the clean scent of baby soap, and took her hand in mine when I saw that her almond-shaped eyes were glistening.

She sniffed, swallowed, and eventually asked, "Alors, vous le trouvez comment?" *So, what do you think of him?*

Our full attention returned to the (small) elephant in the room, with his blue onesie and his tawny skin that was a perfect blend of Kalahari's ebony skin and her husband's Mediterranean tan. His face looked kind of bunched, like he was pissed that we were interrupting him in his drooling and doing nothing.

My mouth worked in vain for a second, until I turned to March. "Why didn't you tell me?"

"I figured you'd enjoy the surprise," he replied, his voice unexpectedly shy. He too seemed awed and kind of intimidated by the mysterious creature.

"What's his name?" I inquired, poking one of the baby's feet gingerly—and retrieving my hand just as fast when it curled in response.

"Samuel. Well, Sam for short."

"He's . . . full of hair, and fingers," I noted, inspecting him. Sensing a compliment was needed, I added, "He's a very nice baby. How old is he?"

Kalahari giggled. "Not even two months old. I wanted to call you after I was sure, but you were at the Poseidon . . ." Her voice trailed off, a fleeting sadness shadowing her features.

"I know," I murmured. "But what matters is that I'm here now."

"Do you want to hold him?"

I froze. Did I? Apparently, yes, since Kalahari placed Sam in my arms almost as soon. I held on to that light, limp little body for dear life—what if he squirmed and I dropped him? But he wasn't doing much, content to stare up at me in fascination with his big, dark eyes. His brow crinkled in visible effort, and his tongue darted a few times before a renewed stream of bubbly drool started trickling down his chin, then my sweater.

"He loves doing that," Ilan commented soberly.

March winced.

Kalahari clasped her hands. "So, who's hungry?"

I gave her a pitiful look. "Do you have any yogurt?"

•••

Draped in my dignity, I ate the "farandole" of potato purée on my plate—with a little fowl breast, *yay*—while the rest of them devoured the whole juicy beast after some foie gras on toasted brioche, because it was goddamn Christmas. After they were done, Ilan went to fetch a Tupperware he kept on the terrace and opened it to reveal the nastiest, smelliest Reblochon you could possibly imagine. They had fresh baguette to go with it, and I watched him and Kalahari eat half of it with appreciative moans. Pure agony. At least, March wouldn't touch that with a foot-long pole, so he kept me company while Kalahari helped herself to a second slice of cheese and told me how much she had missed that particular delight during her pregnancy.

I could easily empathize . . .

When she winked at March and asked, "Guess what's for dessert?" I broke.

As she placed a creamy, luscious *fraisier* on the table, I balled my fists and announced, "I don't care if this kills me. I'll leave this world without regrets."

March's eyebrows pinched. "I'd rather you postpone dying, if you don't mind. That being said, I don't think *fraisier* will kill you—it might, however, give you a stomachache."

I held out my plate to Kalahari. "Valhalla, I'm coming."

She served me a slice as big as March's with a snorting giggle. I could feel his eyes on me, watching for any sign of discomfort as I gobbled down each exquisite bite. My stomach did hurt a little after I was done, and I felt kinda queasy, but I acted cool and didn't say anything: I didn't want to vindicate him. His own plate was cleaned with deadly efficiency, and he helped himself to a second slice as soon as he was done. I secretly took it as a challenge, but I had to admit to myself that I wasn't up for it. At least, for now . . .

March scraped the last trace of vanilla mousse from his plate and rewarded Kalahari with a beatific smile that matched Ilan's. "Thank you. It was perfect."

"Consider it an early Christmas present," she replied, before tilting her head at me. "Do you want me to do something about your hair?"

My hand flew to my bald spot reflexively. "Oh, you mean . . . Yeah, I tried to comb it over so it wouldn't show too much."

But it couldn't possibly escape the eagle eye of a woman who ruled over not one but two Parisian beauty salons—and sold her own product line. She *tsked* me. "That's the kind of stuff you can't hide, so you need to embrace it."

I stared at her in confusion.

"You need an undercut."

March and Ilan listened in silence, obviously trying to display the appropriate amount of polite interest as I asked, "What's that?"

She rose from the table. "I'll show you. Even Cara Delevingne has one."

That's the precise moment a series of hiccupy sobs burst from the baby monitor sitting on the kitchen island. Kalahari sighed. "I'd been hoping he'd sleep a little longer."

I offered her a compassionate wince. "He doesn't sleep much?"

"I swear he must have been trained by the Mossad . . ." Ilan groaned, running a hand across his face.

Kalahari left the kitchen and returned moments later with her little parasite firmly stuck to her chest again, except this time her shirt was open and a tiny hand rested possessively on her breast. We all followed her to the living room, where she settled between Ilan's legs on the daybed to feed the ravenous beast. Curled against March on the couch, I watched them with a mixture of tenderness and curiosity. Back in New York, most of my friends were too young—or too immature—to have kids, and I myself was an only child, so I can't say I had been given the opportunity to study that many babies in my short life. Kalahari would sometimes grimace and shift to a more comfortable position as little Sam chewed on her nipple mercilessly . . . but she looked happy, oddly serene even though her beautiful apartment was littered with crumpled paper towels—that March had insisted on picking up for her—and she probably hadn't had a full night's sleep in two months.

I looked down at my lap, where March's hand held mine, stroking it absently. His expression was soft, relaxed as he watched Kalahari and Ilan, but let none of his thoughts through. Did he find kids scary too? Especially miniature Mossad agents trained in sleep-deprivation techniques? He had a few years on me—almost a decade, in fact—and it sometimes crossed my mind that we were in different places in life. Would he, someday . . . maybe when we're older? When we ran out of ways to risk our lives? As I pondered this, his lips brushed my temple and pressed a kiss there, like a silent reassurance that we had a life ahead of us to make our own choices and mistakes.

But I wanted to at least cage dive with great white sharks and go on one of those real haunted house tours before I'd consider taking on the ultimate challenge of child-rearing.

Meanwhile, a satisfied burp marked the end of the ritual feeding. Sam rested on his father's shoulder, his eyes half-closed as Ilan patted his back to elicit a second burp. That one geysered out Michael Bay style: behind me, March stiffened as Sam regurgitated a trickle of milk and drool on the cloth Ilan had placed on his shoulder for this very reason. Of course, his sweatshirt got stained anyway, because babies *aim.*

Kalahari sat up to take her little demon back while Ilan wiped his shoulder. He sent a look March's way and mumbled, "Faut s'y faire." *Gotta get used to it.*

She got up from the daybed and wiggled her brow at me. "Ready for your haircut?"

I rose from the couch with a firm nod. "Okay, I'm in."

She nuzzled Sam's curly hair fondly. "Tu vas rester avec tonton March pendant que Maman joue à la coiffeuse. Oh oui, on va bien s'amuser avec March!" *You're gonna stay with uncle March while mommy plays hairdresser. Oh yes, you're gonna have fun with March!*

The interested party paled. "Kalahari, I'm afraid I'm not qualified, and can't possibly provide the level of fun you—"

She cut him off with a laugh. "Come on, don't be shy!"

I had almost forgotten this detail: she could be ruthless, especially with March, whose bullshit and intimidation tactics had no effect on her. She all but shoved Sam into his arms, forcing him to catch the projectile with lightning reflexes. He held his "nephew" at arm's length for a couple of seconds, before gingerly bringing him to his chest. And he looked . . . panicked. I couldn't remember having ever seen March so stiff and awkward, as if he feared that the merest movement would somehow break the baby and trigger a series of catastrophic events until sirens blared in the distance. That, or he worried that the next burp might geyser all over his shirt. His usually unflappable poker face bordered on a cringe as the tiny creature started to squirm, possibly reaching for his nose. Said nose quivered, and its owner lowered his head cautiously to sniff the baby's lower half.

March sniffed again, this time more insistently, and so did Ilan, who stepped closer. March eventually attempted to hand the child back to his mother. "Kalahari, I believe he . . ."

She dodged him to latch onto my arm instead. "I'm thinking we can turn that bald patch into a hair tattoo; you're gonna love this."

"I . . . uh . . . what?" I looked back and forth between her and March, whose distress appeared to be increasing by the second. "Well maybe, before that, we could—"

"Come. Let's go to the bathroom for that."

"For what?"

"For your haircut."

"*Chérie* . . ." Ilan pleaded in his turn.

But it was too late; she was already dragging me toward the set of double doors leading to her bedroom and, from there, the bathroom. The doors closed behind us, leaving March and Ilan stranded in the living room with a baby in need of a new diaper.

I blinked at her while she rummaged through a massive closet to retrieve a large red vanity case from one of the shelves. "Are you sure we shouldn't help . . . with the diaper?"

She shrugged. "It'll do them good. I'm on diaper duty 99 percent of the time. This, right now, is my 1 percent, and believe me, I'm going to enjoy it. To the fullest."

Meanwhile, I registered a faint knock at the door, followed by March's strained voice. "Kalahari, this child needs your urgent attention."

She rolled her eyes and shouted, "Cry me a river, bad boy. The diapers are in the changing table, with the baby wipes." Then for Ilan, she added. "Epates-moi!" *Amaze me!*

Through the door, I recognized the culprit's much deeper voice as he told March, "Ok, pas de panique. Tiens-le-moi pendant que je vais chercher ma boite à outils." *Ok, keep cool. Hold him for me while I go get my toolbox.*

My eyes went wide, and I whirled around to face Kalahari. "Are you sure he knows what he's doing?"

"More or less. It often gets incredibly complicated when Ilan is the one changing Sam: first he needs a pair of latex gloves, then the diaper won't open so he needs to cut it, then the tape on the new diaper won't stick so he needs duct tape." She shrugged with a tender smile. "He always manages eventually."

"Okay . . ." This child wouldn't survive winter.

She pulled out trimmers from her vanity case and grinned. "Ready?"

And I wouldn't either.

FOUR
PREDATOR

> "'I warned you, Caprice, I never lose sight of my goals!' he roared. She stepped back, her heart tap-dancing deliriously under the confines of her tight bustier. No man had ever wanted her enough to place cameras in her apartment. Such was the inescapable power of Dante Fenix."
>
> —Jazzmeen Fury, *Winds of Lust*

"It's . . . interesting."

"You don't like it?" Sitting on the couch, I bit my lower lip and kept my head still while March inspected the results of Kalahari's efforts. The feeling of his fingers threading in my hair sent delicious shivers coursing down my spine, which did contribute to alleviating my self-doubt to some extent.

"I do. I didn't expect this, but it does look very sophisticated."

"Of course it does. I'm a pro," Kalahari gloated while little Sam snoozed and drooled in Ilan's arms.

I did like it. I just worried that it was maybe too hardcore for someone like me. But it was a great idea: she'd trimmed my nape, and with a razor and some mad skills, turned my bald spot into some sort of tribal design that was half-hidden by the hair on top, and which you could reveal by lifting the curls. Very edgy.

March caressed the bristles on my nape, careful to avoid the inch-long scar that was still healing. "There's a bit of a punk vibe to it."

"That's my middle name."

That earned me a chuckle. "Certainly."

Yeah. Next time I flipped another driver or helped myself to half a dozen napkins at Subway, I would do so with the confidence of those who lived on the fringe of society.

•••

Time flies when you're doing nothing, lazing around on the couch and binging on episodes of *Albator*—or rather *Captain Harlock*, for purists. Ilan had been a fan as a child, and that passion had never really left him: he had box sets of the '78 and '84 seasons and all the movies. Night had fallen, and the cloudy winter sky was now a deep-purple blanket illuminated by the shimmering lines of the Eiffel Tower. At Kalahari's feet in his baby beanbag, Sam appeared to be doing crunches while space-pirate Albator blew up enemy ships.

Around eight, his parents made an unsuccessful attempt at putting Sam to bed, which ended with ferocious wails and quite a lot of pedaling and kicking the air. Defeated, they placed back their little bundle of hate in his beanbag chair, and he calmed instantly, happy to observe us while we ate a late snack—mine consisting of soup, water, and inner tears while Ilan ordered paninis and salads for three. After we were done, March checked his watch and placed a hand on my shoulder. "Your father will land in less than an hour; we should start heading to the airport."

In an instant, the fear and the longing I had suppressed all day returned full force. This was it. Forty-five minutes from now, we would be reunited. March and I hadn't discussed it again since the phone call, but I knew that my little world was about to tilt on its axis: I couldn't keep up the charade any longer, and one way or another, March was about to officially become part of my life . . . which entailed that my father would have to shoulder the weight of at least some of our secrets—I was never telling him March had once put me in his trunk though.

I got up from the couch on shaky legs. "Okay. Just give me a second to grab my coat." I knelt by Sam and patted his leg gingerly. "Good-bye, you. Try not to drool too much; I think your dad is running out of clean T-shirts."

Ilan's shoulders shook in breathless laughter as he picked up his drool machine. Kalahari pulled me in for a hug and caressed my newly cut hair before she whispered in my ear, "He's good with duct tape. He'll make a great dad."

I felt my cheeks grow hot as we parted. "I guess, I mean, maybe . . ." I mumbled.

Did I mention earlier she was ruthless? Because she was. Visibly reveling in my discomfort, she went on with a coy smile. "Enjoy all the sex first, though! You're at the honeymoon stage; it's the best part, when you fuck through value packs of condoms."

Ilan nodded in confirmation, and I'm pretty sure I lit up like a red light while, next to me, March cleared his throat. "Thank you, Kalahari . . . for welcoming us."

She pecked his cheek. "Don't kill too many people on the way to the airport. And I'll be waiting for my call tomorrow: I want to know how it goes."

He took a sharp breath. "Hopefully well."

She patted his chest tenderly. "He's going to love you."

I didn't miss the lines of worry that appeared on March's brow as she predicted this. He might have seemed cool and totally prepared, but I realized that he too was nervous about what was at stake. How this evening played out would determine whether we could hope for a normal life together . . . or if I would have to make a choice I didn't even want to think about.

After we'd said our final good-byes and the Citroën's doors slammed shut, he leaned back into his seat and drew a long sigh, his gaze lost past the Eiffel Tower's gilded silhouette.

"Are you okay?" I asked. "You look tired."

He shook his head. "No, don't worry. It's just that . . ." I waited while his jaw worked in silence. He eventually turned to me. "They have a baby."

"Yeah, I noticed," I replied in a giggle.

March waited for me to fasten my seat belt like he had and then turned on the ignition. "I suppose that seeing him was a bit of shock . . . because it made me aware of the passing of time in a different way. I never realized Kalahari was no longer twenty-three until today," he concluded with a faint smile.

"And you figured you're no longer twenty-four either?" I asked tentatively.

He ducked his head. "In a way."

"It made me think about Beatriz and Antonio's daughter too. Is she born yet?"

"No. It will be at least another week until my Twitter feed is polluted with ugly animated gifs and baby pictures." He smacked his tongue in disapproval. "I should never have accepted to follow him."

I bit back a laugh because he looked genuinely annoyed, but I would have to find out what Antonio's Twitter was ASAP. I had to witness that storm of crappy gifs.

It was a quick drive to Roissy past rush hour, and before I knew it, we were on the freeway, lampposts flashing by in a hypnotic ribbon. We exited into an industrial area away from the main terminals and toward a smaller airstrip I figured welcomed private jets. The parking lot was almost deserted, and when I stepped out, I noticed a dark shape driving across the runway, its lights gleaming softly in the night mist. I drew a trembling breath that fogged the air around me. Was it him?

March noticed too. His lips curved. "Right on time."

My pulse picked up as he led me through the small and quiet terminal. Under the dim lights, a couple of businessmen waited for their own flights on long leather sofas, drinks in hand. I barely spared them a glance. My legs worked faster and faster, until I was running past glass doors and onto the darkened tarmac. Breathless, I sprinted, grew wings, and flew toward the lone shadow stepping down the airstair. I didn't need to see his face, and he didn't need to see mine either. He hurried down the final steps and started running too.

I felt his arms around me and smelled his cologne as he pulled me into a crushing hug, like when I was a child and he pretended he was a monster who specifically ate tummies, like that sunny day in October when they lowered my mother's casket in the ground and I just couldn't take it. He murmured my name, sniffed hard, and I realized he was crying. It was his tears and mine mingled on his cheek, his fingers in my hair, and mine digging into the soft scarf around his neck. He pulled away, just enough to cradle my face in his gloved hands. Through the glimmering sequins blurring my vision, I saw the pale blue eyes I knew, the mustache he liked to think made him look a little like Burt Reynolds.

His thumbs wiped my tears, and he caressed my hair over and over. "Don't cry, baby girl. I'm here now; it's gonna be okay."

I nodded, my throat too tight to let through any sound.

He was smiling, but the crow's feet at the corners of his eyes and the lines around his mouth were deeper than I remembered. He had lost weight too. Those eight months spent mourning and hoping had taken their toll on him.

As he patted my cheeks, the corners of his mouth fell down all of a sudden. His eyes narrowed, staring past my shoulder. At March. He let go of me, but his hand lingered on my back protectively. "Is that him?"

"Yes."

"Mr. November . . ." he said, in a voice so cold I barely recognized it as his own.

March nodded. "It's an honor and a delight to meet you, sir."

My dad took a step forward and froze. "Cut the crap. Are you armed?"

"No."

March's answer surprised me almost as much as my dad's question. I hadn't noticed, but he was right: the black holster I was used to seeing under his jacket appeared to have been missing all day. It meant nothing and everything; it squeezed my heart and made me smile. "It's okay, Dad . . . I told you he wasn't dangerous."

"Island, honey, you don't know him like I do. Believe me, this man is hiding terrible things!"

My eyebrows shot up in sync with March's. What the hell? How could he already know? Phyllis would have never said a single word without March's prior approval, I was certain of that. She was too smart to let anything slip. So, maybe Murrell or someone from the DOJ? I couldn't picture a former CIA agent like Murrell shitting all over a classified file the size of March's, and the guys at the DOJ probably didn't even know he existed.

March tilted his head, gauging my father with unreadable eyes. "Did Agent Murrell tell you that I was . . . 'hiding terrible things'?"

My dad waved an angry finger at March, and I reckoned that his invisible rotor was now spinning fast. "Do you think I'm stupid? I've seen that video like everyone else!"

I looked back and forth between the two of them in complete confusion, which only deepened when March replied, "And I am profoundly sorry you had to witness that, but I'd like to stress that those were very specific circumstances—"

"You killed three men!" my father roared.

Blood froze in my veins—not because of the three guys, obviously. I had no idea how many people March had killed over the course of his career, and I tried to overlook the fact that he probably didn't know either. "Can anyone tell me what's that . . . video?" Sweet fricking Raptor Jesus, if there was *any* public trace of March's exploits, I could kiss my dreams of a white-picket fence and family Christmas good-bye.

March cleared his throat. "There's been a minor leak of the incident on . . ." He flicked his hand up to indicate the sky. On *Odysseus.*

I felt blood drain from my face. "Oh. My. God. How . . . *minor?*"

"Anecdotic." Reading the disbelief in my eyes, he quickly added, "Island, you had just woken up, and I didn't want you to worry about this. I can assure you it won't be a problem."

Just as he said this, my father pulled out his phone, his face pink with barely controlled rage. "You and I don't share the same definition of what a problem is, Mr. November." He swiped across the screen to load a specific file and pressed play with a dramatic tap. "Honey, I know you've been through a lot, and I'm sorry," he said with a grunt as the video started. "This is difficult to watch."

I braced myself for the worst when Yayleaks's logo appeared on-screen. It soon faded out to reveal regrettably high definition footage of what I recognized as one of the twelve sections of *Odysseus*'s ring. Three guys seemed to be talking to each other, but there was no sound. Two of them wore the white space suits of the orbital ring's rotation crew: they'd turned on the US government to become Anies's minions and killed the rest of the crew to make room for him and his Lions. The third one wore a black suit and had a gun—a Lion, indeed.

Power went out all of a sudden in the section, and the phone's screen turned near black . . . before the camera switched to night mode, revealing a fourth man. Whose face had been conveniently replaced by a Predator's head. *Hilarious* . . . The Predator—let's call him that—twisted one of the guy's necks so hard his head nearly came off before he used the dead body to shield himself while he shot another guy in the head and the third first in the knees, then in the head too. My eyes darted to March's impassible poker face. I cringed.

After my dad had stopped the video, I went for the obvious angle of defense. "That's, um, horrible. But what makes you think it could possibly be—"

"I received a call," my dad ground out, his eyes firing lasers at March.

One of March's eyebrows rose. "A call? May I ask from whom?"

"An anonymous caller who, like you, appeared to know a lot about me and my daughter," my dad shot back. "He told me that there was no use calling the police or the FBI, that you were protected at the highest level, but that . . . from one concerned father to another, he thought I had a *right to know.*"

March and I exchanged a look. A guy old enough to call himself a father, who knew a lot, about a lot of people, and had taken five minutes out of his busy schedule to throw one last banana peel in the way of his favorite hit man. How reassuring to know that Erwin's old ass was doing well . . .

My dad's nostrils flared. "You're not denying that this . . . is you?"

The Predator raised his palms in a pacifying gesture. "Mr. Halder, I perfectly understand how such incomplete footage could be subject to misinterpretation. Why don't we find a more comfortable place to sit down and work through your concerns together."

Unfortunately, March's nerves of steel and well-rehearsed lines only served to inflame my dad further. He took my hand and attempted to drag me away. "I'm not going anywhere with you. I only came here to take my daughter back! Stay away from us!"

I resisted and freed myself. "Dad, please stop and listen to me. I already *know* about all this."

His features pinched in an expression of betrayal. "But you didn't know about the video."

"No," I conceded, sending a glare to the culprit. "But I knew . . . what kind of job March did. I've known since I met him."

My dad's face decomposed, almost literally so. He went from shock, to horror, and finally, the ghastly pallor of a living dead. He remained mute for several seconds before the usual scowl returned to his features, and he simply asked, "But what is it that Mr. November does, exactly?"

FIVE
APOCALYPSE NOW

"Brook no opposition with Dr. Mackibbin's Arch-Disciplinator And
Helico-Rotary Parenting Harness."

—Alan Tyers, Gin & Juice: The Victorian Guide to Parenting

So, what was it that Mr. November did, exactly? Mr. November had
an honest answer ready for that question. He looked my dad straight
in the eye and said, "I am currently unemployed."

My hands flew to my mouth at the same time the U word escaped
him. My dad went rigid; his moustache quivered. "But your
company . . ."

"Has been left dormant for the past few months. I'm working on
reopening it."

Visibly reeling, my dad turned to me, as if searching for some
confirmation that he was awake and this was no nightmare. I half-

expected him to keep grilling March about his short-term career prospects as a coping mechanism for the whirlwind of revelations of the past nine hours, but he shook his head slowly. "No, no . . . we'll get back to that later." His posture straightened, and his gaze hardened. "I need answers. I want to know what happened to my daughter."

I took his hand. "I know. But let's go back to the apartment for that." I exhaled a puff of fog. "I'm freezing, and I'm sure you must be too."

He pulled me closer, rubbing my arms and shoulders. "I'm fine. I would have gone to Antarctica to find you if I had to. And you know I hate penguins."

A smile tugged at my lips as an old memory resurfaced: He had taken Janice to the Easter and Falklands Islands for their honeymoon because it was her dream to go there, but he nearly died on Saunders Island—according to him—when a group of rock hopper penguins ganged up on him and started pecking at his legs. The incident had changed him, and he could no longer see a penguin on TV without gritting his teeth.

"I promise there're no penguins where we're going," I reassured him.

•••

The ride back to Ile Saint Louis was a silent, awkward affair. My dad watched us like a hawk from the back seat and kept flashing wary glances at the road signs, then March—clearly, he worried that the Predator might be trying to take us somewhere secluded to snap our necks too, and my repeated claims that we were "almost there", didn't seem to help much.

It was only when the SUV stopped in front of our building, in a well-lit street, that he seemed to relax a tiny bit. That is, until March went to open his door and he bristled all over again, stepping out of the vehicle with careful, controlled movements as if maneuvering around a savage and unpredictable beast. March's chest heaved, but he contained his sigh as he took my dad's suitcase for him and showed him into the lobby.

After an elevator ride so tense you'd think it was a filmed social experiment, we finally closed the apartment's doors and gathered in the living room. My dad settled in an armchair while I sat across from him on the couch, clasping my hands together in an effort not to fidget.

March made his way toward the kitchen. "Would you like something to drink, or perhaps to eat, Mr. Halder?"

"Sparkling water," my dad grunted.

"Anything for you, biscuit?" he asked.

I shook my head with a nervous smile. We were barreling fast toward disaster: the mere use of March's favorite pet name for me was enough for my dad's jaw to work in silent anger . . . I took deep, slow breaths, mentally flipping through a manual on how to land helicopter parents in a crisis situation. Let me tell you that there weren't that many chapters, and they all said: "Your dad hates your boyfriend, and he's going to napalm him. Good luck."

Moments later, March returned with a *sealed* bottle of San Pellegrino and a glass—I suspected he meant it as a statement that he would *not* poison my dad. He sat by my side on the couch, and a deafening silence fell onto the living room, only troubled by faint sloshing sounds as my dad poured himself a glass. He drank with slow gulps and eventually slammed the glass back on the coffee table, signaling he was done.

He crossed his arms over his suit and breathed hard through his nose, his eyes traveling between me and March. I realized with a chill of panic that I had seen him pissed at pretty much anything and anyone a zillion times, but until that day, I had never seen him *fricking mad.*

I gulped. "Where do you want to start?"

His stony expression wavered, letting through raw anguish. "Honey, *what* happened?"

"I was kidnapped during the destruction of the Poseidon," I said matter-of-factly.

He nearly jumped from his seat. "By Dries?"

Of course. He'd seen the news like everyone else, the careful campaign orchestrated by Anies to frame his brother and get rid of him. All my father knew was the official version, that Dries had bombed a commercial airliner and the Poseidon, killed hundreds of people in a matter of days, and died in the destruction of the dome . . .

"No. He's dead," I managed out, feeling March's attentive gaze on me. "It was his brother, a guy named Anies. He was the one behind . . . everything."

My father leaned forward, his head tilted in confusion. "Everything?"

"It's a long story . . . that started before I was even born."

Over the next couple of hours, my father paced, sat back, drank the entire bottle of San Pellegrino, and paced some more as I told him *everything*. Okay, not really. My tale skipped a lot of details—like the fact that Alex, the nice ex-boyfriend my dad had been placing so much hope in was a CIA agent, a traitor, a one-eyed psycho thanks to Dries's intervention back at the Poseidon, and . . . dead.

I was relieved to see my dad's attitude toward March shift as I painted him as this mysterious hero who worked for the US government and who'd looked for me for eight months until he'd found me, freed me, and battled bad guys onboard *Odysseus* to save the world. I told him what Anies had done to me, showed him the scar on my nape, at the center of Kalahari's hair tattoo, and his tears shattered me. I left out the space part though and vehemently insisted that Yayleaks had it all wrong: Anies's evil plan had been foiled *before* the ship could take off. I mean, supervillains launching stolen spaceships? Come on!

My stomach sank as I also omitted the fact that I had been the one to kill Anies. I would take that with me to the grave and live with that scar, those few abominable seconds I could never wash away, never undo . . .

In my father's eyes, distrust gave way to shock and, ultimately, a spark of genuine gratitude when I recounted that March had also been the one to save me from my mother's burning car on the day of her assassination by one of Anies's goons. And ten years later, when he had heard through the grapevine that my mom's past was catching up with me, he had flown to my rescue again, fought the bad guys, helped recover the legendary Ghost Cullinan, and generally been cooler than James Bond—and also a total gentleman.

Yeah, I kinda glossed over the whole kidnapping thing, or the fact that March was Dries's disciple and therefore . . . You know. Let's call it poetic license. I chose my words carefully and, once more, took more shortcuts than a keyboard when trying to explain how March and I wound up being dragged into Anies's attempt to destroy Dries: I mostly made it sound like a series of unfortunate coincidences. I could tell my dad wasn't buying it, and I started sweating hard when his eyes narrowed and his brow furrowed, and furrowed some more . . .

Already, I could hear the ominous droning of the rotor.

His pale irises scanned March, no longer angry but intrigued. "I'm getting the feeling I'm missing something here. I don't fully understand why you were there when Léa died, or why Dries insisted on dragging you into his mess . . ." I slowly shrank into the couch's cushions as he went on, nodding to himself. "I took note that you created your business about a year ago and that you've been involved with the US government on three separate occasions since, as some sort of . . . contractor. What remains unclear to me is what you did before that. Were you already working for them?"

I should have known that my dad's analytical mind would be my undoing. I balled my fists as March remained silent, his goddamn poker face letting nothing through. My father cleared his throat to indicate he was waiting for an answer. March rose from the couch. A thousand ice cubes cascaded down my back when I recognized in his eyes the cold-killer look I hoped I'd never see again. Pure, dark ice.

He gave my dad that courteous, soulless smile he reserved for clients . . . "Simon."

I jumped a little at his use of my father's first name, and my father too seemed to perceive the change; his expression grew guarded.

March went on. "I believe Island did her best to explain the situation to you, but I'm afraid she forgot a few details. Will you follow me to the bedroom, please?"

I shook my head silently, fighting back tears. I didn't want him to tell my dad. What if he couldn't understand? If he freaked out and asked me to choose? I couldn't do that. I could *never*.

My father's gaze searched mine for answers, for any sign that he shouldn't follow March. "Island?" was all he said. There was no need to elaborate. *One word from you and I'm taking us out of here, just give me a sign . . .*

I took a calming breath and nodded. "You need to hear what he has to say."

•••

They spent fifteen minutes in there, which sealed the rest of my life. When he came out, my father was white as a sheet, and I read a mixture of relief and regret in March's eyes. It was done. March never told me exactly what he'd said to him, and my dad never mentioned that conversation again either, not even to me. Like Anies's lifeless body floating in zero gravity among black pearls of blood, Dries's identity, my mother's career . . . March's former life became our secret, and I was overwhelmed by guilt that I'd forced my dad into this ugly covenant.

He staggered back to the living room, let himself fall into his armchair, and leaned forward to rest his head in his hands, massaging his scalp.

I approached him tentatively and knelt by his chair. "Dad?"

He drew a ragged breath. "I need a steak . . . and weed."

March and I looked at each other. I hesitated to make him repeat that, for posterity.

March checked his watch. "We can probably find a restaurant open at this hour in Châtelet. As for your . . . other request, I'm not certain that's—"

My dad's head snapped up—by the way, he was right: with that dark look and the moustache, he *did* look a little like Burt Reynolds. "Don't you of all people goddamn *dare* lecture me about marijuana."

March cleared his throat. "No, of course, not . . . obviously, no."

My dad got up and grabbed his coat without a word. It was only once the three of us were standing in front of March's car that he pulled me into a tight hug and whispered in my ear, "I love you so much, honey. But why couldn't you stay with that nice boy from Washington?"

I kissed his cheek. "He lied all the time. March was honest with you."

My dad avoided March's gaze as he broke our embrace. "I think I would prefer a liar, or even a Sociology major, at this point."

•••

I don't remember the name, but it was one of those typical Parisian brasseries: a warm, cozy, and noisy place serving the holy trinity of French restaurant food 24/7—steak, oysters, and *croque-monsieur*, of course. It was past 1:00 a.m., and diners were becoming scarce, replaced by nocturnals who would drink and smoke on the terrace for a couple hours more under umbrella heaters.

In a quiet corner of the room, March and I watched my dad tear through a twelve-ounce tenderloin steak and its side of french fries, all washed down with a few glasses of Pinot Noir.

He gulped down a mouthful with an appreciative grunt. "That's the one thing the French know how to do well. Worst bankers I've ever done business with, but they always take you to great restaurants to seal their deals." He toasted us absently and finished his glass. "Christ . . . I haven't had a steak in three weeks."

"Is Janice still into veganism?" I asked.

"It's getting out of control." He dragged his chair away from the table to show us his shoes. "See this? That's not leather; that's some kind of PVC they make with recycled tires."

My jaw went slack. "Wow."

March pursed his lips in appreciation. "Very nice."

My dad paused in his eating to stare at him weirdly. "I eat tapioca every goddamn day, and I wear recycled tires."

Sensing he'd committed a faux pas, March immediately sobered. "And I am terribly sorry for you, sir."

Nodding to himself, my dad went back to his french fries. "I love her, but we can't go on like this." He looked at me. "Did you know there's milk and eggs in pancakes?"

"Um, yeah."

"Well now she's making them with soy milk, and she tells me it tastes the same," he said somberly.

"I've read almond milk is an excellent substitute as well," March remarked.

In my father's hand, the steak knife sliced angrily into the remaining piece of meat. He sent me a pointed look. "I liked that boy from Washington."

SIX

THE PIGEONS

"He spread out his wings, blinding her with the pure white of his feathers, the perfection of his sculpted body. She crumbled to her knees, ready to worship his divine staff."

–Lily Lion, Succumbing to the Billionaire Archangel

Maybe I should have counted how many glasses he's had, I thought, as my dad staggered out of the brasserie. I had occasionally seen him buzzed, but certainly never drunk enough to demand that my former-hit man boyfriend go buy weed for him, "from those boys over there," whom he noted appeared to be smoking some.

He waved a few crumpled bills at March, forced them into his hand, and pointed again at the little group of guys chilling—and yes, smoking—on the ledge of the Fontaine des Innocents.

"Dad, you can supply an entire frat house for 350 euros!"

"Good."

March placed a friendly hand on his shoulder. "Simon, we should take you home."

My dad clasped his hand over March's and glared at him. "You want to be part of the family? Go get me some."

"Dad!"

And in spite of my outrage, March did as he had been told—a touching testament of just how much he wanted to please my dad. With a sigh, he walked up to the boys and engaged in a lengthy negotiation. The group's leader, a lanky teen with a black parka, kept waving his hands and seemed to become agitated as March repeatedly shook his head. The guy eventually relented and handed March . . . the whole bag. I followed my dad as he wobbled toward them to claim the prize.

Our dealer shook his head in disbelief and asked March, "Attend, c'est tout pour ton reup? Mec, c'est chaud, là . . ." *Hold on, it's all for your dad? Seriously, man . . .*

March declined to comment, and the guys stared in awe as my father dragged me toward the nearest red-lozenge sign of a tobacco shop—because now, he needed "a helluva lot of paper."

I'd like to reassure you that my dad did not ultimately smoke two ounces of cannabis in one single night. I think he rolled three joints, maybe four, as we strolled together up Rue de Rivoli and all way to the obelisk towering over Place de la Concorde. Bathed in the coppery hue of public lighting, the Ferris wheel stood still, and the food trucks were closed. A few taxis and trucks still circled the place, part of the murmur of the city at night. I huddled against March to keep warm while my dad emptied the rest of the bag of weed on the sidewalk, "for the pigeons." It was three in the morning, and the temperature was under forty, so no, there weren't any pigeons.

He didn't want to head back, so we found a bistrot and settled there, drinking coffee while all that weed and Pinot wore off. Toward five, my dad lumbered to the restroom—presumably to throw up. As soon as he was out of sight, I scooted closer to March and stole a brief kiss. "I'm really sorry about this."

"Don't be. He's been through quite a shock, and I think he's sobering up anyway."

"I've never seen him trashed like that . . ."

"Yes. He was"—March's lips twitched—"quite lit."

I stifled a giggle in his shoulder and felt him nuzzle my hair, before he stopped all of a sudden. I straightened up. Across the room, standing near the bar counter, my father was watching us. He returned to the table, now more or less sober—albeit somewhat disheveled. A thoughtful waiter had left a glass of water and an Alka-Seltzer on the table. He dropped the tab in the glass and watched with a blank expression as it fizzled. "We will never mention this again," he rasped—did he mean March's job, or how he had distributed a bag of weed to imaginary pigeons? Leaving me to speculate, he brought the glass to his lips and chugged it down with a grimace. He slammed it back on the table and fished a copious tip for the waiter from his wallet. I didn't dare remind him that you don't tip in France, and when you do, you drop a two-euro coin with a regal flick of your wrist like it's a hundred-euro bill.

March and I stared at him in silence until he took his coat and simply said, "Let's go home, honey."

•••

We went back to the apartment to have breakfast, shower, and change. Phyllis arranged a flight for us and told me she'd be waiting for us at Teterboro. It felt good to hear her voice: I stayed on the line a little longer while March packed his suitcase and my dad called Janice in the living room.

"So how's the reopening going?" I inquired, sprawled on the bed.

"Smoothly. We'll be back in business in no time. After all, he's a legend now!"

Hair prickled on my scalp as I remembered Ilan's passing comment that March was a "living legend." "You mean that video?"

"So you've seen it?"

"Yeah, my dad showed it to me."

She marked a pause. "Ouch."

"Yeah . . . *ouch*."

"Don't worry too much. March made a few calls to share the pitch of his memoirs and asked if he should consider leaking them too. Believe me, the idiot who uploaded that is in a lot of trouble . . ."

I felt bad for the idiot in question. It was just a stupid joke, after all . . . "But I don't want anyone to get hurt," I whispered in the speaker. "I just want to know there won't be . . . more."

"There won't be. Our legend actually gained a lot of leverage from that disaster with *Odysseus*. There aren't that many people who'll try to go after a man who knows what he knows"—her voice dissolved into a warm laugh—"and who destroyed a spaceship! Oh my God, I still can't believe it. I wanted to put it in our new brochure, but it was a *no* from March."

"I think it's better this way," I said firmly.

Her voice softened. "I know. He wants to reassure your father. How did it go?"

My eyes darted to the hallway where they both stood, ready to go. *Night and day, the hyper-anxious banker and the glacial hit man.* For a second, I thought I saw Dries instead of March, and I felt my eyes grow hot. "I think it's gonna be okay."

"See you in a few hours."

"Yeah."

SEVEN
LIVING A LIE

"Zane tore his eyes away from her plump ass with a frustrated growl. His bear could no longer live this lie: of course, he wanted honey!"

–Lane Tempest, *Morning Woods Shifters #1 - Bear to the Bone*

We were supposed to take off from Le Bourget. That is, if we ever reached it. Stuck in traffic somewhere northeast of Paris, we watched the sun rise over clusters of cracked gray buildings—they never show you the suburbs in all those tourist pics; guess why . . . I stretched with a long yawn and caught my dad's tired gaze in the mirror. He sat very straight in the back seat, his fingers rapping on his lap as our SUV slowed down behind a delivery truck. I itched to tease him about that crazy night, but I sensed it was too soon: he had yet to fully recover and come to terms with everything he'd learned.

"There's a bed in the plane," March said with a smile I'm pretty sure my dad misinterpreted as some sort of carnal invitation, judging by the way his moustache twitched.

I wrapped my hands around my body and rubbed my arms, yawning some more. "I can't wait."

An insistent buzzing coming from the back seat had me twist my neck to check on my dad as he took out his phone from his coat pocket. The mask of mild annoyance he had retreated behind ever since leaving the apartment became surprise, then concern as he took the call. "Yes, it's me. I'm still in Paris." His blue gaze set on me. "Yes . . . She's with me."

My stomach knotted in sudden anxiety as he offered me the phone. "Honey, Joy wants to talk to you."

Until that very moment, the life I had left behind back in New York had been a blurry horizon made of faces, places, and memories. As much as I wanted it back, I felt disconnected from it . . . like an old movie whose characters seemed familiar. But Joy's soft voice calling my name suddenly made it real. "Island, is that really you?"

I wish I could have come up with something better than, "Hey . . ." but my breathing was too shallow, my throat too tight as it all rushed back to me: Joy helping me stalk a guy in her civil law class, Joy ruining our microwave with a miscalculated Gummy bear fondue recipe—yeah it should have been the chocolate in that bowl . . . Joy buying Malibu and cupcakes to comfort me after March broke my heart.

"Oh shit . . . " She whimpered. "Are you okay? Please tell me you're okay!"

"Yeah, I'm peachy." I sniffed back tears and noticed March's right hand frantically searching the glove box for a tissue pack, which he gave me. I took it with a trembling nod.

On the other end of the line, I heard her blow her nose much like I was. "Everyone thought you were dead . . . Your dad texted me that you fell into a coma when they pulled you out of the dome, but when you woke, you had amnesia, and no one could figure out who you were for months!"

I stole a glance at the chief screenwriter in the mirror and swallowed hard. He had wasted no time starting to smooth out the way for my return. As uneasy as I felt about the precarious web of lies we were tangling ourselves into, I had to admit it was a pretty solid story . . . Guilt weighed in my chest like a bag of rocks at the idea of keeping Joy in the dark, but I couldn't see any other way. March wanted—needed—a new life, and it came at the cost of burying the old one. For good.

"Don't worry. It's all over now. I'm coming home," I said in a brittle voice. Neither a lie, nor a denial of my father's explanations . . . It would have to do.

"Is it true that Valmont is the one who found you?" Joy asked, relief and astonishment coloring her voice.

Valmont? Manipulative French viscount with a wig? "You mean March?" I clarified, remembering the nickname she'd once given him. "Yeah, he found me, and he brought me back."

She seemed to hesitate before she replied, "So he's a PI, right? Back when Thom died, he was investigating something with you in Switzerland? Before the Poseidon."

"Yeah, he's . . . kind of a PI."

"I get it. Your dad said you land at ten in Teterboro. I'll be there. So, don't disappear again!"

As she finished, a sleepy mumble rose from the phone. "Babe? Who you talking to?"

"It's Island! She's coming back!" she whisper-shouted—to Vince-the-cutest-photographer-in-the-world, I presumed. It was weird and maybe a little disheartening to think that he had moved in with her after they thought I was dead. I realized for the first time that, technically, I no longer had a home to return to: I didn't live there anymore.

I shook off this depressing thought and instead tried to reassure Joy, "Don't worry. I swear I'm not leaving that airport without you. So it's you who'd better be there, otherwise I'll have to set up a tent in the lobby, and maybe security will show up to kick me out, and I'll have to use the extinguishers to fend them off."

For the first time in eight months, I heard her bubbly laugh. "Okay, now I know you're really back. I'll see you in nine hours." She paused and drew a sigh before adding in a brittle voice, "I love you, girl. I could seriously propose right now."

"I have a boyfriend," I said automatically.

She sobered. "I know. I guess I misjudged him . . ."

I noticed that March had pulled onto a smaller street lined with hangars bearing aviation companies' logos. "I gotta go; I think we're at the airport. Get ready for my swag; I'm almost home."

"I'm so ready," she purred in her best sultry voice.

I hung up and gave my dad his phone with a sorrowful smile as March parked in front of the terminal, a low building surrounded by taxis and luxury cars awaiting travelers. "Thank you for what you told her. I know it's not easy."

March's eyes met my father's in the mirror. "I'm very grateful," he said.

For a second, his brow lowered, and I feared he'd explode again, but he breathed out his anger, and his lips quirked. "I've been pretending to be a vegan for over a year . . . my life is a lie already."

•••

It was only after the door had closed that I realized there was no control panel, no buttons to be found on the elevator's wall. I couldn't remember why I had entered it in the first place, what I was doing here, or where it was going. I spun on my heels and tried to escape, but the doors had already slammed shut. *Oh shit . . .* My heart ramming against my ribs, I felt the car move with ominous creaking sounds. I braced myself, filled with the inexplicable certainty that it would fall. I waited, waited in that cramped space that seemed to be closing in on me. But the elevator kept going. It wasn't falling.

I backed away slowly, up to the wall, noticing for the first time that there was no floor indicator. The car stopped with a jolt, and the lights went out. I screamed in complete panic, banged at the cold brushed-steel walls. I called March's name, my dad, over and over until all I could produce were barely audible croaking sounds.

Exhausted, I fell to my knees and curled in the dark, blind and alone. I cried.

"Island . . ."

My head snapped up, and I blinked frantically, catching a flash of red in the darkness. I felt him. His breath against my neck, the smell of the absinthe. Somehow, he was here, with me. I picked up a rustling sound and groped at the air with trembling hands. My fingertips met skin and something hot and sticky. I recognized the scent of blood, and suddenly I was weightless as the elevator fell, and Anies lunged at me, bathed in red light.

I howled my lungs out and clawed at his face, his chest. His blood was transferring onto me, covering me, drowning me. But I kept fighting.

"Island!"

My eyes fluttered open, and my stomach heaved at the feeling that everything was spinning around, the cabin's walls, the seats. I was in the bed. No. On the floor, tangled in the blanket I had fallen asleep under. It wasn't Anies struggling to block my furious kicking—it was March, his body curled around mine, his hands caressing my hair, his breath in my ear. "It's over, biscuit; you're safe."

My father too was kneeling next to him, stroking my leg with a shaky hand. "You had a nightmare, honey."

I propped myself up on my elbows, taking in the jet's cabin. March's tablet rested on one of the seats, the crosswords app still open. Two pillows lay on the floor, which I'd sent flying in my desperate bid to escape Anies's ghost. I let myself fall back in March's welcoming arms, feeling nauseated by the cold sweat that made my sweater stick to my back. I could still feel him crawling under my skin. I couldn't escape Anies yet; I carried him with me.

I let March help me up and into one of the seats while the blond flight attendant I prayed I hadn't inadvertently kicked went to fetch a glass of water for me. "I'm sorry," I mumbled as she offered it to me.

With each gulp, I could feel March's and my dad's eyes on me, dark and light, but filled with the same anxiety. Maybe they had more in common than they knew . . . "I'm okay. I'm really sorry about this."

March gave me the soft smile I needed so much right now. "We'll be landing soon. You're going to see Joy."

My dad sat next to me and pulled me into a hug. "Janice has prepared your room, and I've kept all your things."

I noticed the flash of surprise in March's eyes, soon followed by resignation. Something passed between us that didn't need words because I was certain we were on the same wavelength: I had no intention of returning to live with my parents. Which begged the question: where would I live then?

•••

Joy wasn't alone on the tarmac; standing next to her was a shorter, dark-skinned figure wearing a dramatic black-and-white ethnic poncho that I bet was wool-free. Joy ran toward the airstair and hugged me the second my feet touched solid ground. I returned the favor, smothered in her blond curls and the sugary scent of her perfume. As soon as she let go, Janice took over, and I think it was the first time I ever saw her moved to tears. She had no children of her own by choice, but as she smoothed the front of my coat with shaky hands, I realized that there was motherly love in her nonetheless, more so than I had ever suspected.

My dad was next, and *he* got some smooching action, which I'm certain made up for all that veganism. He wrapped an arm around her shoulders and planted a kiss in the silvery frizz that surrounded her like a mist and fell on her shoulders. Her blissful expression turned suspicious though as she lowered her head to sniff his wool coat. "Simon, is that . . . ?"

He cleared his throat, and I noticed his neck was a little red. "No, no. It's synthetic; don't worry."

What could she possibly respond to that? Question the ethics and devotion of a PETA hero? *Well played, Dad!*

As for March, Janice greeted him with a mixture of distance and curiosity. I gathered she had sensed my father's discomfort even through his lies, perhaps on an instinctual level, and it echoed in her reserved, watchful stance. Joy, on the other hand . . .

"Okay, a lot will be forgiven of you because you're hot."

My mouth fell open in horror, and March raised an eyebrow as she scanned him up and down with a frown. "Thank you, Joy."

Her eyes narrowed. "Don't thank me yet. There's a whole host of shit that doesn't add up in Simon's story." When she saw me blanch, her expression softened into a sad smile. "I just hope that someday, when you're ready, you'll tell me the truth."

I remained speechless, as did March. How I ever thought I could successfully lie to a lawyer, I have no idea, but being sort-of-but-not-quite exposed lifted an incredible weight off my shoulders. Joy didn't have to know everything just yet, but she *understood*, and there was no need to bullshit her and enrich my dad's tale with farfetched details. I took her hands. "When we're old ladies in our retirement home in Florida and I'm worried I have to write my memoirs before my Alzheimer catches up with me and also I need to make money in self-publishing because I've lost my 401k in a banking bubble . . . I'll tell you everything. And you probably won't believe it."

She looked down at our joined hands with a grin. "I can't wait."

•••

It's when we reached the airport's parking lot and my dad marched to his Lincoln, fully expecting me to follow, that things became awkward.

"So you're gonna stay with your parents for now?" Joy was asking me, but I got the feeling that she was, in fact, looking at March.

"I, um . . . I haven't really decided."

My dad whirled around and stared at me. Then at March. Then back at me. I felt myself shrink under his disapproving scrutiny. His chest heaved, and he seemed ready to speak, but a dark and mysterious hero stepped into the line of fire to rescue me. "I still have my apartment on Central Park West. You're obviously welcome to stay there, biscuit. As long as you wish."

I didn't dare to beam in front of my father, given how pissed he looked at the moment, but I could hardly contain the joy and relief bubbling in my chest. He'd said the words, made it tangible: we would be living together. With his orange tree!

My dad counterattacked. "That's very kind of you, but Island probably wants to spend time with her family, and all of her things have already been moved to our apartment anyway—"

"I'll help you move them again," Joy offered with a shrug. "Vince and I are having lunch with my parents tomorrow, but I can come on Sunday. We can meet at nine at Simon's place."

Janice gave a firm nod. "And I'll have pancakes for all of you!"

"What do you think, Island?" March asked with a smile that was just a tiny bit smug.

I breathed in, breathed out, and forced myself to face my dad's wounded look. "I'd like that."

EIGHT
HOUSE RULES

"Ricardo aligned his muscular body with hers. His incandescent shaft was so incredibly long and large: how could she possibly take him? He silenced her fear with a sweltering kiss, branding her perfect lips like a hot iron. 'You're the only sheath this machete will ever need, my love.'"

–Kerry-Lee Storm, *Carnal Blaze: A Cost of Rica Novella*

Looking back on it, it was kind of like a divorce: March won full custody but had to promise to deliver me to my grandparents' house on Long Island at six sharp, so I could spend Christmas with my family. *He* wasn't invited, because I'd just come back after eight months of anguished waiting, and it was way too early to introduce a boyfriend into the equation, what with the shock that would cause my grandpa, who was eighty-seven and whose doctor said he had bad coronaries!

Under the pretense of fatherly concern, my dad even managed to throw a jab about March's ability to support me, since he was after all *unemployed*, and he had "a few holes in his résumé." See? Just like a divorce.

I'd forgotten what New York under the snow looked like, felt like. Paris died a little in winter, grayed and withered until mid-March, and even a glut of lights and Christmas ornaments couldn't fully hide that cyclical decline. New York inexplicably thrived under the snow. Cars got jacked up with rust; salt cracked under your boots and got literally everywhere. You learned to survive without vitamin D and came up with coping strategies when the blizzard blew so hard you couldn't even stand straight. At dusk, you walked past a bum curled up in his sleeping bag in front of a Burger King, and you were left with that tiny prickle of guilt in the pit of your stomach for the rest of the night.

But then dawn came, you blinked, and suddenly, you saw beauty everywhere, in the delicate, shimmering crust of ice on the sidewalk, the soft white mantle covering Central Park like Chantilly swirls. There was the clatter of the horses' hooves and tourists taking selfies in the carriages, the sweet aroma of the hot chocolate at the Russian tea room, or even Rolf's Christmas-decorations extravaganza . . . And you realized that this, right here and now, was the most romantic city in the world after all.

I spent the entire ride from the airport taking it at all in, like a kid at Disneyland. March would look at me every time we stopped at a red light, with tenderness and curiosity. But he said nothing and let me soak in the colors and the sounds, content to just be here with me.

Impermeable to time, weather, or family drama, the 111 Central Park West stood as tall and proud as ever, with its brick-and-stone façade and Beaux-Arts ornaments—nothing too tacky though. It was the kind of place you wrote ghost stories about, I mused as March and I passed the revolving doors. All brass and marble, guarded by an elderly concierge and his young apprentice, both standing behind a long desk—they had a nice white Christmas tree too.

No doubt honed by decades of experience, the concierge remained perfectly deadpan, greeting "Mr. November" with a slight tilt of his head. The young guy with the mohawk however, made no attempt to conceal his shock, blinking awestruck eyes at March. "I thought you'd never come back, Mr. November! Were you doing time?" he asked with a noticeable Caribbean accent.

His old mentor cleared his throat at this candid—but somewhat legitimate—inquiry while March walked to their desk with a chuckle. "No, Delroy. I wasn't in jail. How have you been?"

Delroy adjusted his wine-colored jacket with a smug grin. "Out of trouble."

"Excellent." The corners of his eyes crinkled, as if he'd just remembered something. He pulled a bill from his wallet, which he gave to Delroy. "Do you believe you could bring me my usual?"

"Jumbo crosswords and Killer Sudoku?"

March ducked his chin. "Exactly."

"You got it, Mr. November!" the guy cheered before he leaped over the desk and ran past me, leaving his colleague in a state of mild consternation. Maybe because Delroy persisted to wear light-up sneakers with his uniform.

Once we were in the elevator, March's fingers flew to a small touch screen, entering the code that would grant us access to the fourteenth and fifteenth floors—respectively Struthio's office and the penthouse I would live in for the foreseeable future.

"So you're into Sudoku too?" I asked.

"Yes. I find it immensely satisfying."

I rested my cheek against his chest with a smile. "Everything in its rightful place."

"Something like that."

The elevator bounced to a stop on the fourteenth floor, and the doors opened to . . . a stack of boxes, and behind them, a mop of fiery red curls. Phyllis hopped from behind the pile like a jack-in-the-box, perched atop black stilettos and wearing a strict white blouse and slit pencil skirt.

Her face lit up as soon as she saw me, and she maneuvered around the boxes to look me up and down, her arms akimbo—was she that tall the last I'd seen her, or was it the heels? March and his six feet three barely had an inch on her. "Struthio Security never gives up on a case," she said with a radiant smile.

I stepped forward and gave her an awkward hug, unsure whether it was appropriate since March was her boss and she was, after all, at work. But she returned it without hesitation—dammit she *was* tall.

"Thank you," I breathed, "for everything." For the months spent morally supporting March while he recovered from his wounds, for handling his business after his "death," all while investigating my whereabouts for him . . . for being so much more than his assistant.

She patted the box closest to her. "New brochures have arrived! Want to take a look?"

I gave an eager nod while she ripped the tape sealing the box and retrieved a glossy booklet. The emu had been adopted for good: it was back on the cover, peering directly into our souls with an angry orange glare.

"It's premium paper," March commented proudly as I started reading.

Is your chief accountant being held hostage in Nicaragua? Have your employees disappeared with strategic data or assets? Are you being blackmailed for any amount in excess of $500,000? Then you need to think smart, act fast, and strike efficiently with minimum collateral damage: you need the power of an ostrich! Struthio Security provides high-end services to companies or individuals facing critical security issues and immediate threats to goods and personnel. Act now! Call 111-OSTRICH or visit struthiosecurity.com to learn more about how we can help you.

Phyllis pointed to her chest with perfectly manicured nails. "And I wrote the pitch."

"Very powerful," I praised, my lips pursed in admiration.

"Flip it around, biscuit," March instructed, an undercurrent of boyish excitement in his voice.

I did as told, and my mouth immediately bounced into an admirative O. I flipped the brochure over and over, watching the wings of the ostrich logo flap. "You got hologram printing?"

"Just a little marketing gimmick," he exulted quietly.

Phyllis winked at him. "And I already have a few inquiries I need you to take a look at. No time off for you, Mr. November."

I was happy for him and, of course, relieved at the idea that we would soon be able to reassure my dad that "the boyfriend" wasn't some sort of dangerous moocher—far from it, in fact. But it also made me realize how fast real life was catching up with us, when we hadn't even unpacked yet . . . I think March sensed the tiny speck of disappointment I was trying to suppress. He told Phyllis, "Send those to me please. We'll see if they're urgent or if they can perhaps wait a few days."

So we can have time together. Just the two of us. Just a little time . . . I resisted the urge to leap into his arms and French him in front of Phyllis.

He picked up our suitcases and tipped his head to the flight of stairs at the end of the hallway. "For now, let's get you settled, biscuit."

"Okay."

As she heard this, Phyllis's eyebrows arched, and she held up a finger at March. "Before I forget." She hurried toward a set of padded doors, and when she opened them, I glimpsed Struthio's office, with her glass desk covered in perfectly organized stacks of papers, all labeled with color-coded Post-it notes. She returned with what seemed like a several-page document, which she gave March.

He took it with a nod. "Excellent, thank you." When he saw me peek at the cover in curiosity, he handed it to me. "Phyllis printed a welcome brochure for you."

Being no stranger to the lengths March could go to control everything and everyone in his environment, I beamed, even as warning signs lit up one after another in my mind. "Oh . . . really? You shouldn't have."

"You deserve no less," he replied, perhaps a little stiffly.

I started leafing through it as he led me up the stairs. The "welcome brochure" was, in fact, an endless list of draconian house rules ... from the color of our respective toothbrushes to his elaborate laundry routine or the mandatory use of slippers everywhere in the penthouse except in bed and inside the tub—where those were forbidden—every aspect of our future cohabitation was covered in excruciating detail. The kitchen towels and dishcloths too had a color code—so one wouldn't be mistaken for the other. The brochure said that, for everyone's safety, I should be extra careful not to dry my hands with a dish cloth, or worse, wipe the sink with a hand towel—because the sink must be wiped clean after each use, first with an antibacterial wipe, then with the appropriate microfiber cloth.

I read again that paragraph about kitchen safety, wondering if there was a thinly veiled threat behind March's choice of words, or if maybe something truly horrendous would happen if I accidentally misused the microfiber cloth. I envisioned an elderly cop with a fedora and a trench coat looming over my body while paramedics drew a sheet over it. Then a rookie would take a cautious step toward him, avoiding a pool of blood, and the old cop would pull out a cigarette and mumble, "Wrong towel. It's not pretty."

So yeah, my heart thumped understandably a little faster as he turned his key in the lock and opened the doors. Light poured from the windows in the absence of any curtains, showcasing the stunning view of Central Park I remembered. The penthouse was spacious enough as it was, but with so little furniture and the white sheets covering it, the place looked even bigger. I recognized the shapes of March's couch, floor lamp, and a single bookshelf against a wall. In the kitchen area, the sheets concealed a long table and a single dining chair.

The sound of March clearing his throat stopped me before I could take another step. I looked down, following the direction of his gaze. Slippers, of course. Fighting a blush of embarrassment, I removed my boots and put on the white hotel slippers awaiting me next to the doormat. He did the same and put away our shoes and coats in their designated closet.

Only then was I allowed to continue my tour, examining the second flight of stairs that led to the mezzanine. There too, the ghosts of a bed and desk with its chair sat idly. I realized there was only one thing in this apartment that wasn't covered—or rather, one *occupant.* I don't know if it was because of the suitcase standing next to me, or maybe Phyllis said something she shouldn't have while she watered him, but in any case . . . Gerald *guessed.* I mean, I know it sounds crazy, but the moment I saw him standing in his pot in a corner of the living room, it was as if the air had chilled, raising goose bumps on my back. He knew I was moving in.

Think I'm kidding? Well *he* wasn't: March took my hand, perhaps to lead me upstairs, and at this precise moment, a greenish and disfigured orange fell from one of Gerald's branches and rolled silently across the room. To stop at my feet. I gulped softly as March picked it up with a sigh. The message was crystal clear, and I took a shivering breath at the idea that I would be spending my nights fifteen feet away from a psychopathic orange tree.

"So," March asked, "do you think you'll get used to it?"

I took another circular look at the penthouse. "It's amazing." *And a lot bigger than anything I would ever have imagined myself living in . . .* "I'll pay you rent," I decided. "With the money my mom left me, I'll be able to pay my share."

His eyebrows drew into a mild scowl. "Island, this is ridiculous. I'm not even leasing in the first place, so there is in effect no rent to share, and I don't want you to—"

"And don't make it fifty bucks," I warned him.

March shook his head with a huff that clearly suggested we would have this conversation again. "Come, I'll show you where your closet is."

We climbed the stairs leading to the mezzanine, and I had to stop to admire the view again: you could see the lake even better from here, like a dark-blue mirror surrounded by a delicate brown-and-white lace of naked trees. Behind me, March pulled and folded the sheet covering the bed, revealing blue—and impeccably ironed—linen.

"Have you decided which side you prefer?"

I blinked.

"Page seven," he clarified, gesturing to the welcome brochure.

I flipped to said page. Indeed, it said I was expected to pick the side of the bed I would sleep on and preferably stick to it. "Um . . . you pick yours, and I'll take the other, I guess."

He nodded in confirmation that the deal was sealed, before crossing the mezzanine to open a massive walk-in closet. "I will have doors installed on your side." He gestured at the dozens of shelves—a lot more than I needed really. "This way, you can organize your clothes any way you like, and"—his voice seemed to falter—"I won't know."

New doors to hide my mess? Excellent idea. I gave him a sheepish smile. "Thank you."

"It's my pleasure entirely." After he'd placed our respective suitcases in the closet, March returned to the bed, sat down, and patted the space next to him. Heeding his invitation, I plopped myself at his side. "Now," he began, nuzzling my cheek tenderly. "Why don't we go over that welcome guide together, to make sure that you . . . have all the information you need."

My blissful smile melted into a sour grimace, and at that precise moment, I'm almost certain I heard the rustling of leaves, along with a dark chuckle, coming from downstairs. My head flipped to the glass balcony showcasing Gerald.

"What is it, biscuit?"

"Nothing . . ."

"All right." He delicately pried the brochure from my hands. "Let's start with laundry rules."

No way!

I could think of only a limited number of scenarios that would save me from an in-depth review of March's two-page-long list of laundry rules. Having ruled out screaming for fire or faking a faint, I went for the most appealing option: before he could open his mouth, I climbed on his lap to straddle him and wrapped my arms around his neck, bringing our lips a hair's breadth from each other. "Can we skip the welcome brochure for now?" I pleaded, taking the papers from his hands to place them on the bed.

They scattered a little, and he reached with one hand to gather them into a neat stack, his breath growing short as I pecked his lower lip, his chin, his throat . . . "Are you trying to distract me, Miss Chaptal?"

I pressed my body to his and dug my fingers into his shirt, feeling his muscles tighten under the soft fabric. "Maybe."

I should have known better than to underestimate Mr. Clean. March placed his palm flat on my chest to stop the assault and flashed me a smug smile. "Chapter one: Sorting. We have three laundry baskets, for whites, darks, and colors. Dirty laundry must be sorted in a timely manner, and . . ." The lecture ended in a hiss through his teeth when I started working on the buttons of his shirt—whites basket, of course.

"How about we do this," I offered, raking my nails through what I had officially dubbed the rug of Eros. God, if he ever shaved that chest hair, I'd need victim counseling to recover. "You can sort your own laundry by color, and I'll do mine, like usual."

He tilted his head, and his eyes narrowed. "Island, I know for a fact that you've struggled with dye-transfer situations in the past, and in my humble opinion, the best way to prevent this is . . ." This time, it was my fumbling with his belt that seemed to impair his speech. I put on a remorseful-kitten look, complete with some lower-lip biting, even as the leather traveled through each loop of his jeans waistband. His hands reached under my sweater, helping me pull it over my head. "A color catcher," he breathed in my ear. "I think a color catcher will take care of it."

I pushed him flat on his back, and for a guy who must have weighed about twice as much as me, he didn't resist much. When I "accidentally" kicked the welcome brochure and sent it flying to the floor, his head turned to the scattered pages, and his fingers reached for it reflexively. By then though, I was busy unzipping his jeans, and my own pants appeared to have vanished as well. I saw the conflict playing on his features, until he gave up and closed his eyes with a sigh—maybe because I was kissing my way down that wonderful trail of hair, past his navel, and . . . well, you get the idea.

I remember the point where he couldn't take any more of my clumsy teasing—combined with a bit of clinical examination, for science—and he rolled atop me. We spent a while like this, a tangle of warm skin and limbs, looking into each other's eyes, speaking a wordless language made of kisses, smiles, and, I guess, pheromones. As March stroked my hair and we tethered to the brink of successful intercourse, I realized this was different than our first time together, maybe because there was a little less performance anxiety on both sides. There wasn't so much tension when he had to stop to go hunt for a condom in his jeans pocket—which I had tossed across the room in my earlier enthusiasm.

And even when he returned to me, I was surprisingly chill about the final act. It still hurt a little, but it was okay; I didn't mind. Actually, I felt . . . completely high and liquid. As he moved, I became aware of my body in a new and confusing way, like a buzzing in my lower half that made breathing and thinking difficult. I threw my head back with a blissful—okay, idiotic—smile. My eyes fluttered open. March was watching me, intently, his hand gripping mine tight on the comforter. He barely blinked, transfixed as if there was nothing more important in the world than me writhing and scrunching my face weirdly under him.

I know it's gonna sound weird, but it made me think of the last stage of tetanus, the way every muscle in my body tensed, strained almost painfully. I think I also hissed a few pithy observations and commands such as "Oh" and "Wow" and "Please don't stop!"—March reassured me in a breathless groan that he had no intention to.

When that beautiful storm finally hit, a tiny, remote part of my consciousness noted that, as orgasm faces went, mine was probably pretty bad. Like I had smashed my big toe into a piece of furniture at the speed of sound. While listening to Tan Mom's latest single. In hell. But it was okay, since March didn't look any better, his face twisted in an expression of sweet agony, his teeth clenched so hard I could hear his molars grinding together. I was vaguely aware of high-pitched moans—mine, I guess—and after we crashed back to Earth, I just lay there, gasping for air like a fish out of water, my legs shaking around his.

Best cardio of my life.

Above me, March appeared in a similar state of shock, and under my fingertips, a delicious sheen of sweat made his skin a little sticky. His lips lingered on the damp bangs matted to my forehead until he rolled to his side with a satisfied sigh. I immediately latched back onto him, kissing the salty skin of his shoulder with the fervor of a new convert. My mouth worked in vain as I tried to forge words into coherent sentences. I wanted to tell him it was great—that *he* was great—and everything in general was warm, shiny . . . and great. But he had, quite literally, banged my adjectives away. So, I just asked, "How long is your refractory period?"

Answer: not long, as you might expect of a healthy partner whose primary sources of entertainment over the past five years had been crosswords and a few one-night stands I itched to ask about. The second time was pretty awesome too, but not quite as earth-shattering, which left me a little worried that from this point on, I'd spend the rest of my days chasing my first high like a desperate junkie. Praised be Raptor Jesus, March alleviated those fears with a memorable third round on his bath rug—yeah, we had meant to take a shower, but we didn't even make it to the tub.

The rest of the day was blissfully wasted—in bed mostly—doing Sudoku, making love again, taking a break to pick up our clothes, and cuddling afterward. Also, I'm pleased to say that the welcome brochure landed in my nightstand's drawer, where it should remain sealed until the end of times . . .

•••

"Are you going to fall asleep, biscuit?"

Quite possibly. Soaking in the tub, my head lolling against March's chest and with his arms wrapped around my waist . . . I was in soapy, bubbly, wet-chest-hair heaven. I smiled and let out a soft purr to indicate I was still conscious.

He kissed my temple. "It's half past four. I'm afraid we need to get ready."

I stared at our respective toes peeking out from the foamy water, slowly coming back to reality. The Christmas dinner. March had promised my dad he'd drop me at Roslyn Heights, where my grandparents anxiously awaited my return—no doubt while my grandma cooked enough food to feed a regiment. My lips twitched at the thought of all the Tupperwares I'd go home with before I covered March's hands with mine. "I just don't like that you're gonna be alone again. You've never celebrated Christmas with Phyllis?"

"No. I expect a lot from her all year long, possibly too much. She needs to have this time with her son, her family. Don't worry." He chuckled. "Kalahari never misses our Christmas call."

"Are you gonna tell her about my dad?"

"Do you want some specific details to remain classified?"

I sat up with a laugh. "Nope. Feel free to entertain her."

Once I'd gotten on my feet and was about to climb out of the tub, I realized March had made no move to follow me. Propped on his elbows, he was gazing up at my naked body. Some shred of modesty had me battle the urge to cover myself. I mean, he had seen—and sampled—everything already, but on a subconscious level, I couldn't shake the atavistic response of a virgin girl freaking out that a *guy* was seeing her butt-naked in broad daylight.

His lips curved, pinching two dangerous dimples. I couldn't stop the heat spreading on my cheeks and ears when he rose from the water in his turn. For some reason, the goods looked less intimidating when we were frolicking under the covers rather than . . . on blatant display.

He lowered his head to press a single kiss to the pulse beating fast in my neck. "Cover yourself, Miss Chaptal," he murmured. "Before I make us late."

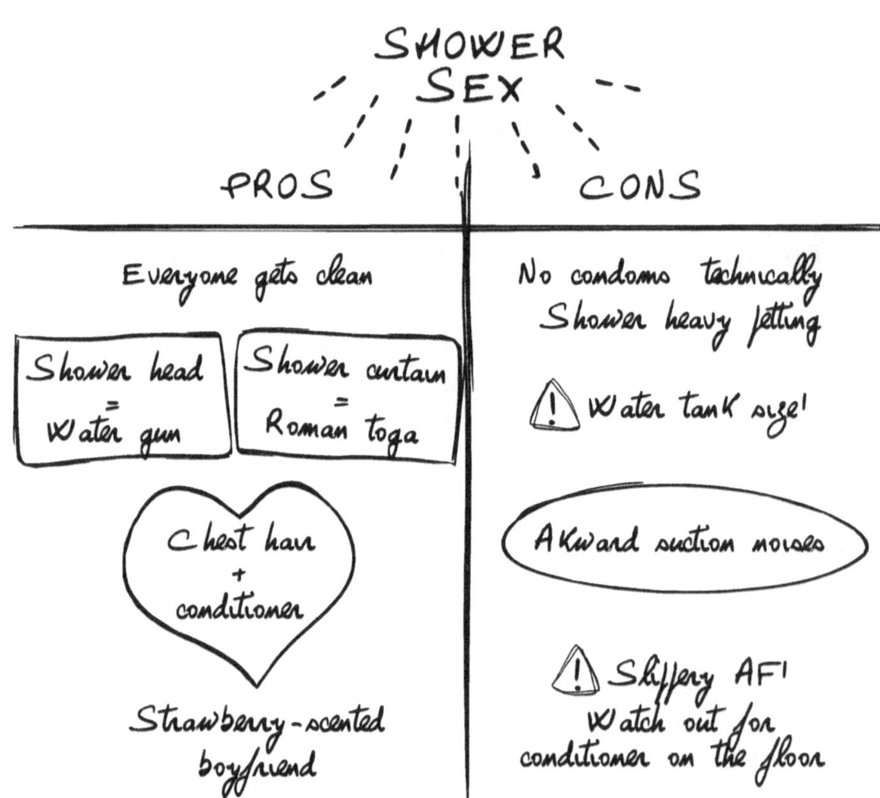

SHOWER SEX
PROS
CONS
Everyone gets clean
Shower head = Water gun
Shower curtain = Roman toga
Chest hair + conditioner
Strawberry-scented boyfriend
No condoms technically
Shower heavy jetting
Water tank size!
Akward suction noises
Slippery AF!
Watch out for conditioner on the floor

NINE
THE BOYFRIEND

"Each torturous intake of air felt like a firestorm in his windpipe. He clasped his hands at his back, digging his nails into his palms. The pain was a welcome distraction from the furious need to tear off her bonnet, right here and now. 'Samantha . . .' he growled huskily, 'will you let me court you?'"

—Tammy Xavier, *Buggy Heat*

He drove me to Roslyn Heights, where a Victorian house stood under an old pine, at the end of Winterberry Lane. My grandma's impeccable lawn was covered with a smooth white blanket that reflected the bright colors of the street's most controversial holiday-light display. March parked in the driveway next to my dad's car, and his eyebrows jerked as he gazed upon . . .

"She pulled out the inflatable Jesus."

"I can see that."

It wasn't just that it was an inflatable and backlit representation of our Lord with a shit-eating grin and a bad case of sausage fingers. It wasn't the grotesquely bloated lamb he held in his arms either. Those constituted serious but nonetheless forgivable infractions in my grandparents' swanky neighborhood. No, the real issue was Jesus's rainbow-colored toga painting the snow all shades of blue, pink, green . . . pure provocation.

My grandma received oral and written complaints every year, stressing the ambiguity of the message this particular display conveyed, and insisting that it made some of her neighbors uncomfortable. But she was eighty-three, she liked her inflatable Jesus, and she didn't give a damn.

March leaned forward to better examine it. "Who needs Jeff Koons when you have this?"

I shook my head with a laugh. "Don't tell her that or she'll set up a lobster too next year . . ."

That etched two dimples in his cheeks, and it made me want to spend the evening in the car with him. March leaned closer to kiss my forehead, the tip of my nose, until our lips met. Even after we parted to breathe, his forehead remained against mine, his voice an intimate whisper between us. "Enjoy your Christmas party, biscuit. I'll see you tomorrow morning."

"I know. I'm just sorry that you can't stay."

"I think it's best to take things slow with your father. Let him have that time with his family."

I nodded, my throat a little tight. Outside, the house's door opened and warm light spilled onto the driveway. I recognized Janice's ample red-silk dress and frizzy silver hair. She waved at the car excitedly and squealed, "They're here!" for the entire street to hear. It wasn't long before the doorway crowded with my father's guarded frown, my grandma's frail silhouette, and, yep, that was my grandpa, wheeling and elbowing his way between them, his poodle on his lap.

My father came out first, closely followed by my grandma. Like a cotton-haired mouse wrapped in a pink shawl, she padded behind him hesitantly, her eyes squinting behind her glasses, as if I were a mere ghost that might evaporate in the night air. But then, a spark lit up in her faded-blue eyes, and she closed the distance to welcome me in her arms, in her shawl that smelled of a sweet old-fashioned rose perfume.

"I prayed every day," she said in a trembling voice. "So they better not call about my Jesus this year," she concluded with a fierce, protective glance toward the ten-foot inflatable Messiah guarding her lawn. Soon enough however, I realized that I was no longer the entire focus of her attention. She tilted her head, looking past my shoulder in a visible effort to glimpse March—who appeared to hesitate between staying in the car and making my dad happy, or revealing himself and satisfying my grandma's curiosity instead.

"Is it him?" she asked.

I nodded.

She waved gnarled fingers at March. "Come out. Don't be shy. I don't bite."

My dad's chest heaved in rising aggravation as March stepped out in his turn and greeted her with a duck of his chin and a smile that could have melted all that snow. "Good evening, Mrs. Halder. It's a pleasure to meet you."

"Mr. November can't stay with us tonight. He's very taken by his work," my dad interjected, in a bid to regain control over the situation.

My grandma's head jerked up, the lines around her mouth framing a scandalized pout. She was even shorter than me, but she towered over my dad nevertheless, dwarfing him with her absolute mom power. "What do you mean he's not staying?"

From the porch, my grandpa yelled, "What did he say?"

My grandma yelled back, "He says the boyfriend isn't staying!"

"Why?"

"Because he's working!"

"Who?"

"The boyfriend!"

This time, my grandpa thought it useful to cup his hands to shout his response—just in case his voice got lost while it covered the thirty feet separating us from the porch. "It's Christmas, and I can see him standing on my goddamn lawn. He's not working!"

While my dad appeared on the verge of apoplexy, and his eyes kept shooting daggers and then missiles at "the boyfriend", my grandma seemed to have made up her mind. She took March's hand in hers and patted it. "Tell me, do you like glazed ham?"

His gentle expression turned apologetic. "Mrs. Halder, I'm afraid that—"

My grandpa's powerful croak cut him off again. "What did he say?"

"He says he's staying for dinner!"

"Good!"

•••

The pineapple-glazed ham was great, and my grandma made a mean strawberry trifle that March wiped from his plate at lightning speed. I'm not gonna lie: This first Christmas wasn't all glittery unicorn poop and strawberry-flavored kisses. It was at times awkward—and frankly tense when my grandparents grilled March about what he did in life. Lies were told. Lots of them, and I'm sorry for that, Raptor Jesus. I know you see everything from above. Anyway, it wasn't so bad: March got his first ugly Christmas sweater ever, at thirty-three—the age of the Christ, like my grandma said. I don't think she did it on purpose, but the sweater featured a giant penguin with googly eyes, and I honestly thought my dad would spring from his chair to strangle March when he tried it on.

First Christmas together? Check.

•••

"So, was it okay for you after all? Not too awkward?" I asked March as we drove on the expressway toward Manhattan. I checked the mirror; one of the few pairs of headlights following us belonged to my dad's Lincoln.

"I doubt your father will forgive me anytime soon for intruding on his Christmas party, but your grandparents were very nice to me—and your grandmother is an excellent cook."

"Don't worry. My dad'll come around eventually, and you scored with my grandparents. My grandpa seemed pretty impressed when you told him to drop his old Remington for a PSG-1. Aren't those expensive though?"

"A little," March conceded. "But you can find used ones under fifteen thousand dollars."

"Wow."

"I'm not a hunting enthusiast myself, and Janice would probably disapprove of this . . . but with a good scope he'll be able to hit a squirrel at a thousand yards."

I chuckled. "With armor-piercing ammo?"

"As long as he complies with state regulations."

I nodded tiredly. I was having a hard time keeping my eyes open as we neared Queensboro Bridge. On the other side, Manhattan's twinkling skyline stretched along the East River, like stacks of diamonds reaching for the sky. King of emos Vincent Van Gogh would have loved the sight . . .

"We've almost arrived," March murmured, noticing my rapidly decreasing state of alertness.

Once we were on the bridge, my gaze drifted to the empty ropeway of the Roosevelt Tram, dangling above the East River. "They're not done fixing it yet?"

In the driver's seat, the man responsible for breaking said tramway in the first place let out a weary sigh. "Unfortunately no. The mayor's office and EMG have been fighting over technicalities for months."

I yawned. "Make sure you show up for the reopening . . . They're gonna love that.

TEN
RAPT

"People disappear all the time."
–Diana Gabaldon, *Outlander*

"Okay . . . it's the last one." Joy stretched with a lenghty sigh after she'd dropped a box full of my collection of troll dolls in the middle of March's living room, next to a haphazard stack of twenty or so other boxes, half of which were filled to the brim with books and comics—all in all, I had enough muscular chests in there to populate my own gym. To be honest, March had carried the biggest part of my treasure, but Joy had insisted on giving us a hand, chiefly to inspect my new lair.

My eyes darted to March, who stood by my side as Joy inspected his lone Chesterfield and the Ikea floor lamp standing right next to it.

He looked a little pale at the sight of the mountain of stuff we'd moved in. I needed to organize it. Quick.

"You don't have a lot of furniture," she told him, trailing a blue-painted nail along the back of his only dining chair. "But your place is okay."

He welcomed the compliment with a nod. "Thank you."

My lips pinched to stifle a laugh. "Okay" indeed. A two-thousand-square-foot penthouse—three thousand including the mezzanine—was absolutely . . . okay. And don't even get me started on the terrace. March had yet to do anything with it, but it had "Island's Barbecue Heaven" written all over it.

I gave March's hand a light squeeze and rolled up the sleeves of my sweater dress. "Okay, I need to start putting all this stuff in my closet."

"Will you need help, biscuit?" March asked.

Before I could answer him, Joy clasped her hands. "I'll do it! This place needs a little mess!"

Avoiding March's anxious gaze, I successfully turned my wince into a smile. "Um, maybe we can just put the boxes away for now. I'll open them later."

He shook his head. "No, no . . . if you want to open them, take your time."

"Oh, those are so cute! Where did you get them?"

Like raptors and four-year-olds, Joy moved fast. Too fast for either me or March to stop her as she leaned closer to his bookcase and examined the collection of African tin cars lined on one of the shelves. She poked one. March's Adam's apple rolled in his throat. "It's a little boring to just sort them by color. You could do something stylish and—"

"Oh no, no, please!"

A blue tin car in hand, Joy stared at me as if my face had just melted off to reveal that I'd been David Hasselhoff all along. "I just wanted to move them a little," she said with a hesitant smile. Her gaze set on March as she placed the car back on the shelf. Between two *red* ones. "I'm sorry . . . I thought they were just for decoration."

I caught the twitch in his fingers as he fought the urge to curl them. "It's all right, you can . . . watch them, if you want."

The car was no longer in its rightful place; there was something awkward hanging in the air as a result, and thank Raptor Jesus, Joy felt it. She walked up to me and pulled me into a crushing hug. "Vince is probably gonna let himself starve if I don't get back to toss a pizza in the microwave." She squeezed me harder and whispered, "I'll call you tonight for a debrief."

"Okay."

She released me to gauge March with wary cornflower eyes. "Do you Instagram your food?"

He cocked a perplexed eyebrow. "I'm . . . afraid I don't have Instagram."

"Okay." She smacked her tongue pensively. "I'll learn to tolerate you."

When his lips quirked, she added, "in a hundred years."

•••

After Joy was gone, March and I contemplated all my boxes in silence for a good minute. Gerald stood in a corner, looking almost dead in the ashen morning light pouring from the floor-to-ceiling windows. I got the impression that he was staring at me weirdly again, and all of a sudden, I missed my old apartment on West 81*st* Street, physically. I leaned against March and took his hand, seeking his warmth to soothe that indistinct ache.

"Do you miss your apartment?" he said softly.

Was I that easy to read? Probably. For him anyway. "Yes," I admitted. My memories were there, my old life. Everything before March, before Dries and Anies. But Vince-the-cutest-photographer-in-the-world had moved in, set up a studio in my old bedroom, and I could never recover that innocence again. It was time to move on.

"I'm sorry for all that mess. I'll get it in order."

"Don't worry—"

I shifted to face him and stood on tiptoe, silencing him with a light kiss. "I know it's hard for you too." Caressing his jaw, I went on. "It's a lot to take in. You've got boxes everywhere, we need to get a second dining chair, and Joy touched your tin cars. Plus, you're worried because you know I'm gonna forget half the rules in the welcome guide, and Gerald is pissed that I'm moving in. I think he's somatizing."

As if to confirm my diagnosis, a soft thud drew our attention to the gnarled silhouette at the other end of the room. A shriveled green lump rolled across the hardwood floor to stop at our feet.

I buried my face in my hands and sighed. "He hates me."

March pressed a kiss to my hair. "No. It's nothing personal. Just the stress, I think. I suppose it's a lot of change . . . for the three of us."

I swallowed. I realized my eyes felt hot, but I wasn't sure if I was crying because I couldn't quite yet let go of the past, or because the future felt too vast, too bright to see past the blurry outline of the life to come, and that scared me.

"Kidnap me somewhere," I rasped.

At first, he said nothing. But then my feet left the floor as he hauled me over his shoulder caveman-style. And he did . . . after he had reorganized his tin cars and cleared the living room.

•••

March adjusted his black leather gloves before taking the Mercedes's wheel, and I loved that. Curled in the passenger's seat, ready to roll in my old *Assassin's Creed* hoodie, I watched the slow movement of his hands, listened to the leather squeaking, like that first time in my bedroom, when I'd been so sure he'd break my arms, but instead, he'd ended up supporting me above the bowl while I threw up lunch's BLT and some Dr. Pepper.

Good times.

I skimmed through his phone's playlist as the engine roared in the deserted garage. My fingers paused on a particular track, and a grin tugged at my cheeks as Jack Black's voice filled the car. *Roadie?* Yup, that sounded appropriate.

"You like Tenacious D? I always figured you only listened to country."

The wheel spun easily in his hands, and a patch of cloudy sky came in sight. "I'm open-minded."

"I don't think that word means what you think it means," I shot back.

"I appreciate the reference, however approximate the citation," March noted as the sedan glided along the Hudson—I made a mental note that the gods were on our side, complicit to our escapade: traffic was unusually light in Manhattan, even for a Sunday. Then again, it was lunchtime and the weekend after Christmas too.

I took on a low, raspy voice to answer him. "I have approximate knowledge of many things."

He raised an eyebrow at me in the mirror; I figured he wouldn't get that one. He wasn't the type to watch *Adventure Time*—or Cartoon Network for that matter. I would have to convert him.

"So, where are you taking me?" I probed, all the while checking the signs. I-95, George Washington Bridge. Teterboro then.

His lips quirked, dangerous dark blue eyes looking straight ahead at the road. "The final destination is always a surprise for my clients."

That little shiver, the millisecond of doubt about his intentions that made my heart rate pick up . . . I loved that too.

Other books in the Spotless Series:

SPOTLESS

(Book #1)

BEATING RUBY

(Book #2)

CRYSTAL WHISPERER

(Book #3)

BUTTERFLY IN AMBER

(Book #4)

(Book #5)

ACKNOWLEDGEMENTS

Let us take a moment here to thank Lindsey Nelson, my editor, who bears with my chronic disorganization and somehow manages to make sense of what I send her, to Amy McFadden, who has been the voice of the series since book one, and gave Island and March a soul, and, of course, to you, dear reader, who soldiered through more than 417,000 words to get to that one scene where they bang like animals. This is your reward; you've earned it.

ABOUT THE AUTHOR

Camilla Monk is a French native who grew up in a Franco-American family. After studying business in Paris, she taught English and French in Tokyo before returning to France to work in digital advertising. A self-taught programmer, she spent ten years building rickety websites for financial companies, before publishing Spotless, her debut novel.

Camilla is now a full-time writer and lives in Montreal, where she keeps a close watch on the squirrels and complains on a daily basis about the egregious number of Tim Hortons.

For more (questionably useful) information, visit:

You didn't expect to find any text here, did you?
And yet here we are, passing time together. Reading.
Oops, there's some more.

Still here?

Go do something else!

Maybe you could read something from a better author:
Ruth Downie,
Lisa Kleypas,
Kayti McGee,
Phoebe Fox,
Mimi Matthews,
Jayne Fresina,
Rose Lerner...
Tons of good stuff out there.

Shoo!